catching kalen

Diamond Dreams Book One
MAYA NICOLE
BRITT ANDREWS

Copyright 2020-21 © Maya Nicole & Britt Andrews
All rights reserved.

No portion of this book may be reproduced in any form without permission from the author, except as permitted by U.S. copyright law.

This book is currently available exclusively through Amazon.

The characters and events portrayed in this book are fictitious. Any similarity to real people, living or dead, businesses, or locales are coincidental.

Cover Design by The Book Brander Boutique
Edited by Aubergine Editing
Proofreading by Proofs by Polly

❦ Created with Vellum

AUTHORS' NOTE

Catching Kalen is a gay MM romance. Recommended for readers 18+ for adult content and language. There are brief scenes and references to parental/spousal physical and emotional abuse.

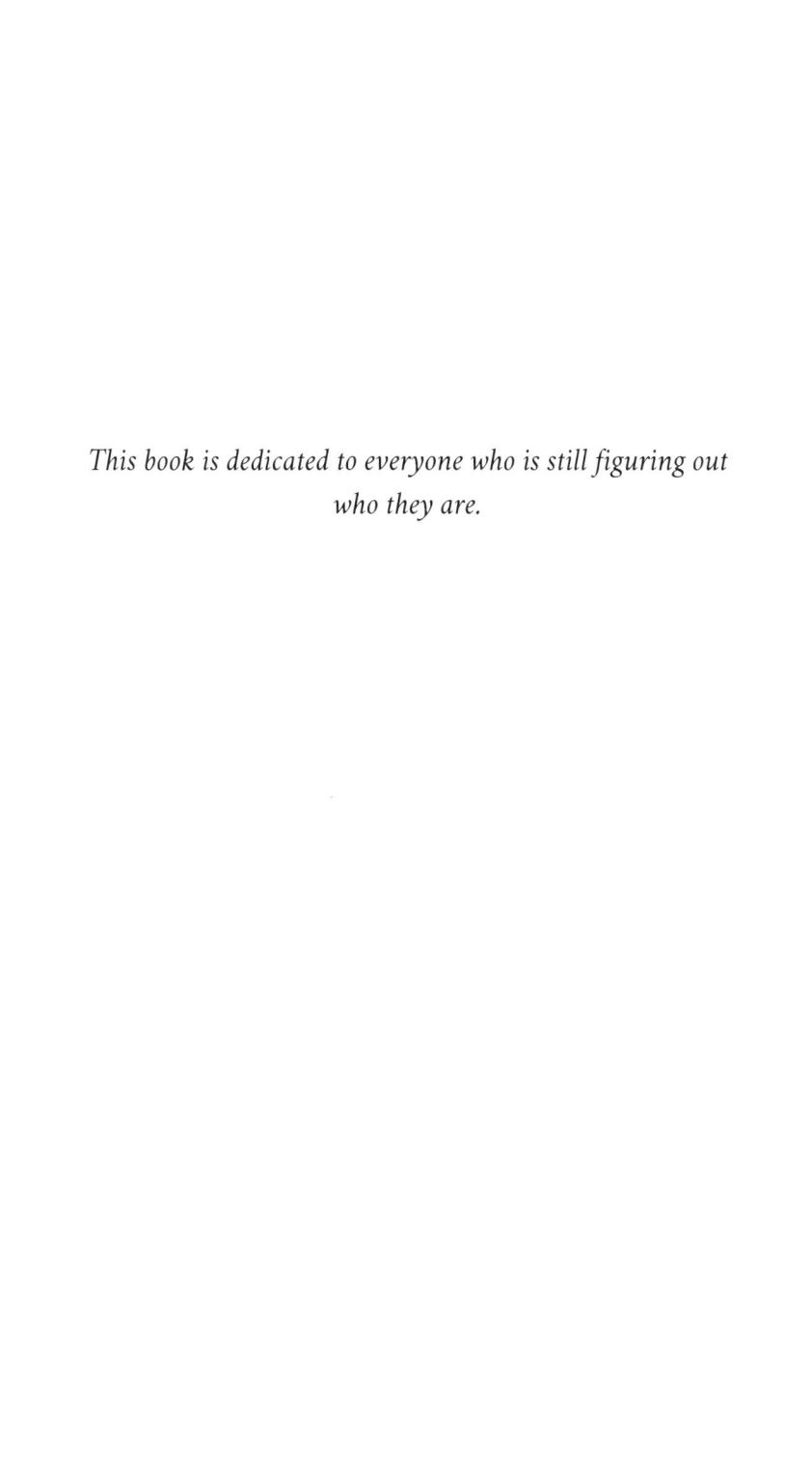

This book is dedicated to everyone who is still figuring out who they are.

CHAPTER ONE

Kalen

"Yo, Bishop! Get over here, man!" Baker shouted across the entire damn bar. He was already seven sheets to the wind; we'd have to carry his ass back to the house later tonight.

Sighing, I snagged my bottle of beer from the bartender, tossed her a five, and dragged my feet over to where nearly all of my teammates had claimed a section of tables, women draped across their laps.

Baker slung his arm over my shoulder. "This is Mandy, and this is her best friend, Sarah. Ladies, this is Kalen Bishop."

Their faces barely registered in my brain as I gave a fake smile and asked how their night was.

Being a well-known college baseball player had its perks, but unfortunately, I wasn't feeling it tonight.

It had been a week, and the sting of not making the draft for the major leagues was still fresh and had me in a shitty fucking mood. Not to mention my summer school class was starting on Monday. *Let's just top off the shit sundae with more shit.*

One of the girls reached out and ran her hand down my bicep. "I've wanted to meet you for a long time. I wear your number to every game."

Looking down at her, I could see she was staring at me like she wanted to throw me down on the table right here, right now, and ride me like her own personal racehorse. Maybe last month I would've been down for that. Shit, I probably would've taken her and her friend back to my room for a seriously fun fuckfest, but my cock wasn't even twitching at this point, and I knew it was a lost cause.

"I appreciate the support. It was nice meeting you, but if you'll excuse me…" I inched away from them as Baker caught my eye and gave me a 'what the fuck is wrong with you' face. He was really good at those.

The music was bumping, and the bass reverberated through the floorboards as I made my way through all the people, making a beeline for the restroom. Maybe splashing some water on my face would help snap me out of my funk.

Just as I rounded the corner, I shoulder checked another guy who had just exited. "Shit, I'm sorry, bro. Didn't see you there." I threw out my hand to steady him.

"No worries, it's all good," he rasped, casually shrugging my hand off his arm.

Well, good, at least he wasn't drunk and going to try and pick a fight over an accidental bump. I'd seen shit jump off in here for way less than that. You just never knew what people were capable of.

Flashing a smile without paying any attention to him whatsoever, I darted into the bathroom.

Come on, Kalen. Get a fucking grip. Not only would I get another year of education—not that I knew what the hell I'd ever do with a communications degree—but I would be the first person in my family to graduate college, and it made my mom so proud to brag about me to everyone she could. Plus, I'd get another year with the top-ranked Division I NCAA baseball team. Deep down, I knew it was probably a win-win for me, but damn, I'd been so sure I'd get drafted.

Hell, I knew I wasn't a first round pick but a few scouts had reached out. After conversations with my coach, we had been fairly confident I'd be middle of the pack.

I needed to man up and pull my head out of my ass. Shit happened, and just because a few teams had seemed interested, didn't mean they'd been under any obligation to pick me. What I needed to do was make them regret not picking Kalen Bishop, starting catcher of a top Division I team.

Jesus, I sound pitiful.

Holding my hands under the faucet, I washed them and then splashed my face in a lame attempt to try and snap myself out of my pity party for one. My green eyes stared back at me, and I convinced myself to count backwards from five and leave it be. No more wasting time.

Five, four, three, two, one. Exhaling, I snagged some paper towels from the dispenser and quickly dabbed at my face before drying my hands. I needed a shot or ten.

When I came out of the restroom, the music was still blaring, and I chanced a glance to where my buddies were sitting practically being mauled by girls. They were fucking loving it.

Leaning my shoulder against the wall, I watched as Thompson pinned a leggy redhead to a post, and she giggled against his neck. Baker was slow dancing with three chicks at the same time, even though the song was a fast one, and I laughed because he was a madman. Usually, I'd be tearing it up with him. Maybe after I downed some tequila.

Sliding my way through the crowd, there was one open stool at the bar, so I helped myself and parked my ass on it. *Since I'm here, I might as well have a double and really get the party started.*

Goddamn, my mood was dismal.

A pause between songs had multiple sports announcers' voices ringing out from the televisions. There had to be fifty of the things. Baseball was everywhere right now, and I just wanted to escape it for a damn minute.

A woman dressed in skimpy, skintight shorts and a red crop top with the bar name splashed across her tits, came to a stop in front of me. I slapped my credit card on the counter with a wink. "Patrón. Make it a double, and open a tab for me, please. Keep 'em coming."

Taking my card, her thumb trailed over mine, and she tossed me a sassy wink in return before spinning on her heel to get my drink.

My boys and I frequented this watering hole often enough that we were regulars, but this was a new bartender, and she was pretty hot. Getting laid wasn't hard, and maybe that sounded cocky as hell, but it was the damn truth. Lately though, every fuck felt the same, and I found myself just going through the motions of the act and wishing for it to be over. Something was missing.

"Here you go, just wave me down when you want another." The bartender's sultry voice was meant to be flirty, but my cock might as well have been dead for all the reaction he gave. *Fuck.*

Gritting my teeth, I nodded curtly and tossed the liquid down the hatch. Before she could walk away, I said, "Two more."

"Bishhhhop, my boy! Come on, bro. We're heading down the street to the club," Baker said, his words slurring. He threw his arm around me, the swaying of his tall body giving me a great indication of how the rest of the night was going to go. I was nowhere near drunk enough to put up with all of their drunken shenanigans.

"Nah, man. I'm just going to chill here for a bit and then head back to the house. You go on, I'll see ya tomorrow." I plastered a fake ass smile on my face, but he still scrutinized it, because it was out of character for me. The whole damn week had been.

"Suit yourself, but make sure you put your headphones on unless you wanna join in later, because there will be sextivities." He wiggled his eyebrows suggestively, and I actually barked out a genuine laugh.

"Sextivities? Dude, get the fuck out of here while you can still walk," I advised, pushing him away as he began fist pumping the air.

Shaking my head, I turned my attention to the alcohol the bartender had set in front of me, drinking both shots quickly. It seemed my countdown in the bathroom had done nothing to snap me out of my funk. Summer school was going to start on Monday and here I was, definitely not utilizing the last of my free time to the best of my ability.

Sex would help. It might distract me enough to—

"Do you want another drink?" A deep voice interrupted my thoughts, and I turned my head to the right; I'd thought all of the guys had left.

But this wasn't one of my guys. This man was older than I was, with thin lines at the corner of his bright blue eyes and a smile that belonged in a toothpaste commercial.

I chuckled darkly. "There's not enough alcohol in this bar, man."

His fingers tapped steadily along the rim of his empty glass as he studied me. His blue eyes were intense, and I could feel my neck getting warmer the longer I was under his examination.

I shifted in my seat as he waved for the bartender. She practically skipped over to serve him, her tits bouncing ever so slightly in her red top. Instead of watching her, he watched me out of the corner of his eye.

"What can I get you?"

"One more for me, and one for him." He tilted his head in my direction. His dark hair fell into his face, and he swiped it out of his eyes.

The bartender looked at me. "Another tequila?" I nodded in response.

"Thanks, man. Just been a long week," I explained to this stranger, who technically hadn't even asked why I was sitting there pounding shots like I was desperate to have the hangover from hell.

He waved me off. "Don't worry about it. We've all been there."

I blew out a breath. "Tell me about it. What's your name?"

His eyebrow lifted, mimicking the corner of his mouth. "Monroe. And you are?" He leaned his forearms on the bar, cool as a cucumber, but there was something about him that made my heart race.

Annnnd that was ridiculous. He'd said like... three things to me, but it was really about the way he carried himself, like he could decimate a man with his brain or some shit. Fuck, the tequila was kicking in.

"Kalen," I replied, as the bartender put our drinks down. Monroe slipped her a bill, telling her to keep the change. He picked up his glass of whiskey and motioned for me to do the same.

"Well, Kalen. What should we toast to tonight? New adventures? Good times?" An emotion I couldn't place flashed across his face, and I swallowed, my throat suddenly tight.

"All of the above," I rasped, pushing my glass

against his before throwing it back, shutting my eyes as the liquid burned going down.

As I opened my eyes, I brought my glass down, and a little drop of liquor slid down my chin. Monroe's eyes tracked its path, and before I could lift my hand to wipe it away, his thumb swiped it off my warm skin.

I sat there, frozen. What the hell was that? Blinking, I glanced around the bar, but nobody was paying any attention to the man who'd just wiped tequila off my face *with his thumb.*

Since I was a glutton for punishment, I looked over at him. He was smirking at me. *Smirking.* All I could do was stare in fascination as he took the thumb that was still wet and popped it into his mouth.

Jesus Christ. My cock twitched in my jeans. I didn't know what was happening, but I felt really hot and confused… and *hot*. I needed to get out of there.

I jumped off the stool before my damn erection got any bigger and I embarrassed myself further. I threw some money down on the bar to tip the bartender. "I think I'm going to head out. Thanks for the shot." My voice was husky and deep.

Monroe picked up his drink and downed the rest of it before standing up beside me. He was maybe an inch or two shorter than I was, but I was a really big dude. He was leaner than me, and I wondered what he was hiding under his gray t-shirt. His *tight* gray t-shirt.

Damn it. What was I even thinking?

"I'll walk you out." He moved past me to the exit, the faint woodsy scent of him making me want to bury my head in the crook of his neck and breathe it in.

"Kalen? You almost forgot your card." The bartender interrupted the tequila-fueled fantasy my brain had concocted, and I pocketed the card before signing the receipt.

I'd been so caught up in Monroe, I'd forgotten I even had a tab open. Or was I drunk? If not, I was certainly on the wrong side of sober.

I turned to find Monroe waiting with his hand on the door handle. His eyes slowly traveled down my body before he opened the door, gesturing for me to walk out in front of him.

Who the fuck was this guy, and why did my cock like him?

CHAPTER TWO

Monroe

The second I'd bumped into Kalen, I knew I had to have him. I'd almost turned back around and followed him into the bathroom, but Slugger's was no gay bar, and I was still getting a feel for how open this college town was.

I'd already convinced myself to pursue him when he came back; his thick thighs and round ass promised a fun time. The thought had my cock straining against the zipper of my jeans, and he'd made it so much easier by sliding onto the seat right next to me at the bar. If that wasn't a sign that he was going to be under me in the next few hours, I didn't know what was.

As I held the door of the bar open for him, he

slipped past me and into the cool night air. I was glad the nights were cooler because it was hot as hell during the daytime. It was supposed to be California, not the Sahara Desert.

He walked toward a bike rack at the edge of the sidewalk and fumbled with his keys. "Fuck. I probably shouldn't bike. Don't want a BUI."

"A BUI?" I'd never heard of such a thing, but then again, I'd never really ridden a bike. Breaking a leg trying to learn at the tender age of five will do that to a person. Real smart decision taking a job in a town that had more bikes than people.

"Biking under the influence. Are you not from around here?" He shoved his keys in his pocket and left his hand there, drawing my eyes not only to the bulge his hand created, but the other bulge right next to it.

"Just moved here." I stepped closer to him, and his eyes widened. "What do you say we go back to my hotel until you're sober enough to bike?"

His full lips parted, and he cleared his throat, his eyes darting around as if looking to see if anyone was watching. The outline of his erection was telling me he was feeling me, but the confused look on his face said something different.

Did I really want to hook up with someone who wasn't sure what they wanted? No, but I couldn't resist a man with green eyes, and his were the perfect moss shade.

"I, uh..." He shifted from one foot to the other, his jeans stretching across his thighs. He was most likely an athlete at the university—he certainly looked like one—but I pushed that thought out of my head.

"What else are you going to do? Go back to your place and listen to your buddy's sextivities?" I ran a hand through my hair and cocked an eyebrow. "Unless that's what gets you off, then by all means..."

"No!" He nearly tripped over the bike rack as he stepped forward, and I reached out to steady him. His eyes locked onto my hand around his muscular forearm and he gulped. "Let's go."

I left my hand on his arm a few seconds longer before trailing my fingers across it as I let go. He shuddered, and I smirked at his reaction. I couldn't wait to run my hands all over him—if he let me.

Leading the way to my hotel which was a few blocks away, I noticed Kalen lingering slightly behind me. "I don't bite. Unless you want me to," I teased.

I slowed down so our strides were aligned, and our arms brushed, sending a jolt of lust straight to my dick. It was already hard at just the thought of him in my bed, but feeling his skin against mine was on a different level.

"I'm not gay, dude." He kept his eyes straight ahead as we turned the corner and the hotel came into view. "I mean... if you were thinking I was."

He had followed me out of the bar and his dilated pupils told a different story. I raised a brow and flashed him a half-smirk. "Could have fooled me." I grabbed his hand and pulled him to a stop, causing his eyes to widen again. "If I make you uncomfortable, don't come to my room with me. I'll get you an Uber or if you're close, I can make sure you get home okay."

He didn't pull his hand away, and his white teeth sank into his full bottom lip. Kalen's gaze landed across the street, staring at some metal sculpture of a bicycle.

Damn, what I wouldn't give to be that lip. I typically didn't go for younger, college-age guys, but there was a spark I couldn't explain, and I had to see how that translated in the bedroom.

"I've never done this." He finally looked at me, and my stomach flipped at the vulnerable expression on his face.

Fuck. Maybe I'd read him completely wrong and he wasn't as into this as I'd thought. The bulge in his pants could have been from thinking of someone else. Someone with tits.

"It's been a really shitty week. I should have known going to the bar was a bad idea." He ran a large hand down his face and then grabbed the back of his neck.

I wanted to ask him questions about what he hadn't done and why his week was so bad. But that was opening a can of worms that would kill the mood. Had he never had a one night stand? Never been with a man? Not had sex at all?

"Do you want to go up to my room or not?" I stepped closer, and he backed up against the side of the building we were next to.

Letting his hand go, I put my palms flat against the brick wall on either side of him. He gasped and his eyes immediately fell to my lips. He was playing hard to get, was he? Maybe he'd never done this before, but it was painfully obvious he wanted to. He just needed a little more coaxing.

I licked my bottom lip and ran a finger along the collar of his shirt. Leaning close to his ear, but not touching his skin, I rasped, "When you're ready to stop playing games, I'm in room two-sixteen."

The ball was in his court now. He would either follow me or go home to listen to his buddy's *sextivities*.

It took a lot for me to push off the wall and walk toward the hotel entrance instead of kissing his fuckable lips. Lips that would look great wrapped around my cock.

I stepped into the elevator and pressed the

button for my floor. To my dismay, it wasn't like the movies where the man rushes across the lobby yelling, 'Hold the door!' thrusting his hand in like a gallant knight to stop it from closing.

Sighing and closing my eyes briefly, I leaned back against the wall as the elevator made its short ascent to the second floor. I couldn't wait to move into my new place on Monday and be out of the hotel. It had only been four days, but I wanted a kitchen again. The truck with all my belongings wouldn't arrive until Monday afternoon.

Stepping into my room and taking off my shirt and shoes, I kept on my socks because hotel carpet is gross. I grabbed the television remote and was just about to sit down when there was a soft knock at the door.

My stomach fluttered; it was such a foreign feeling that I wondered if the tacos I'd had for dinner were bad. I knew it was *him* though. I didn't do feelings when it came to men. I'd tried once in freshman year of college, and it had been a train wreck, leaving me with a broken heart and an avoidance of relationships.

Cursing under my breath, I stalked over and pulled open the door to find Kalen with his hands braced on either side of the door frame, his shirt riding up just enough to show a sliver of tanned skin and a dark shadow of hair leading into his jeans.

This man was grade A all-American beef, and I planned to devour him.

His eyes landed on my naked chest, and then he looked past me into the room. "Are you going to invite me in? Isn't that usually how this works?" His voice was deep, and it didn't escape my notice that it was shaky.

I stepped out of the way, just enough for him to squeeze through. His chest brushed against mine, and I inhaled his scent. Fuck, he smelled like expensive cologne and a hint of tequila. In one word, temptation. He smelled like fucking temptation.

Slipping the *Do Not Disturb* sign on the outside door handle, I let the heavy door swing closed. I turned to find him across the room at the window, looking out at the street. His body was a work of art with strong shoulders and a waist that tapered in just the right amount, leading to his pert ass.

Our eyes met in the window reflection as I walked up behind him. I slid my hands around his waist to rest on his stomach, feeling the ripples of his abs through his shirt. I buried my face against the back of his neck, inhaling the faint scent of aftershave and leather.

"You smell so fucking good." I trailed my lips across the back of his neck to his ear. "I can't wait to sink my teeth into your ass," I whispered as I moved my hands under his shirt and traced the contours of his abdomen. He must spend hours working out for a body like this.

He trembled as I moved my hands up to his chest and slid my thumbs over his hard nipples. His breath was already speeding up, and I smiled against the soft skin right below his ear before licking the shell of it.

"Jesus." He stumbled forward a foot and put his hands on the window. The windows had privacy film on the outside, so I wasn't worried someone would see him. Not that I cared, but he might.

I moved my hands down to the bulge in his pants. He groaned as I palmed him through the fabric of his jeans. He was thick, and I bit the lobe of his ear. "A dick like this is meant for my fist."

He put his forehead against his arm as I unbuttoned his jeans and slipped my hand inside. Precum was already leaking from the tip as I ran my hand down the velvety, hot length of him.

"Please," he mumbled into his arm as I used my other hand to push his pants and underwear down enough to free his cock. "Oh, fuck," he panted as I gripped him at the root and squeezed.

"Tell me what you want, Kalen." I began jacking him off, my fist pumping him, gathering precum from the tip, and using it as lube. I freed my own cock and moved in behind him, sliding against his crack.

He stiffened. "I can't... Not what you're thinking."

"Not tonight, but eventually this ass will be mine." *Eventually?* I kissed along his neck again, one hand still sliding along his cock, the other back under his shirt, teasing his nipple. "Give me your mouth."

He made a strangled sound in the back of his throat, and angled his face toward me, giving me access to those sweet lips that I'd wanted since he walked in the door.

CHAPTER THREE

Kalen

What the fuck am I doing?

My mouth was being plundered by the sexiest guy I'd ever seen, and my brain felt like it was moments from exploding. I'd never in my life had a reaction like this to a man. Never kissed a guy, never jacked off while watching gay porn, and yet here I was, getting my dick squeezed by a man.

As though Monroe sensed my inner turmoil, he slid his free hand up to my hair and gripped it in his fist, pulling back slightly to pull my lips from his. Fuck, why did the sting on my scalp feel like a promise of things to come?

"Kalen," he purred, pumping my cock with the expertise that only someone who owned a dick could have, because damn it if it wasn't the best hand job I'd ever had. "Look at me."

My eyes crashed into his, and I swallowed harshly at the intensity. I bet I could have a whole discussion with this guy without him ever opening his mouth; his eyes were just so damn expressive.

"Does it feel good? Having my hand wrapped around your big dick? Do you like feeling what you do to me?" he questioned, pressing his hard cock against my ass and causing me to groan. *Jesus Christ.* "Answer me, Kalen."

"Yes, yes it feels amazing," I panted as his fist twisted over the head of my shaft.

"Then stop thinking and fucking enjoy it, big guy. I'm going to make you come harder than you ever have in your life. Get these clothes off and get in that bed," Monroe ordered, and I practically whined when his hand left my cock bouncing in the air, unattended.

Tugging off my shirt and stripping down without facing him, I nervously rambled, "I just, this... I've never been with a guy before. Shit, I didn't even realize this was something that I'd ever consider doing..."

When I sat my ass on the edge of the bed and glanced over to see Monroe advancing on me without a stitch of clothing on, my mouth went dry, and all rational thought evaporated from my head.

His physique was very different from mine; he was still obviously in great shape, toned and lean. Where I was built like a professional baseball player, he had more of a runner's frame. There wasn't a chest hair in sight and only a thin smattering of hair trailing from his belly button down to hair that was trimmed short and neat. Though that wasn't what had me clenching my ass in fear... or was that anticipation?

Monroe was fuckin' packing. I mean, I'd felt it against me, but the beast was unleashed now, and fucking hell. He stepped in between my legs, and he pressed up on my jaw, closing it as he chuckled. Apparently, I'd been checking him out so hard I was literally gaping.

"You're pretty sexy yourself, Kalen. Look at this body," he breathed to himself, his hands running down my chest to my pecs and over my nipples, which were almost as hard as my dick. Releasing a shaky breath, I brought my own hand up and let it rest on his hip.

"I know you're nervous, and I'm not going to lie, the thought of being the first man to suck on this beautiful cock has me on edge already, but I'm not going to force you to do anything you don't want to do. But I'm really hoping that you'll let me taste you, Kalen. Is that okay?" Monroe asked, sincerity shining through his lust-filled eyes. My cock was already weeping, and the need to get off was all I could think about.

My mind was at war with itself. I had never even thought about a man in a remotely intimate way.

"Yes, fuck, Monroe. Suck my dick."

What in the holy hell... Apparently, I'd lost my fucking mind when my name wasn't called for the draft.

A sly, heated grin tugged at his lips before he leaned in and pressed his mouth to mine once again. Our tongues collided, and all of my earlier reservations were now gone. I was fucking doing this, and with that renewed confidence, I returned his kiss with desperate urgency.

When Monroe nudged me to scoot back on the bed and lie against the pillows, I did. Oh my god, I did. And when he covered my body with his and his dick rubbed against mine? Jesus, I nearly shot my load all over myself like a fifteen-year-old.

"Your cock feels so good against mine, Kalen," he rasped, leaning up slightly to grab both of us in his hand. He slowly pumped his hand up and down, stroking us with the same rhythm. It was erotic as hell, and my balls were already pulling up tight against my body.

"Fuck, man. Shit. I can't keep up with that, I'm too close, it feels too good," I gritted out between clenched teeth.

He released us and his lips found my neck which

he expertly nipped at and sucked on. The pleasure of everything overtook me and the next thing I knew, I had a handful of his smooth ass in my palm, and I squeezed it in encouragement.

"Gotta taste you. I'm going to lick you so good..." His sinful mouth moved down over my chest, leaving a line of fucking fire in its wake. I was going to burn alive.

"Shit," I cursed when his hot breath fanned over my wet cockhead.

"Look at how hard you are for me. I've been hard as a fucking rock since you bumped into me on your way to the bathroom at the bar earlier." His finger stroked down my length, causing my entire body to break out in goosebumps. How was this man making me feel more alive than any woman ever had?

"Damn, I'm sorry. Like I said, rough time. I wasn't paying attention to anything—" My words died in my throat when his lips pressed against my pubic bone.

"Shhh, I'm going to make you feel good," he promised.

Oh, how he kept that promise. *Holy shit.* I didn't even get a moment to respond to his words before my entire length was buried in his hot, wet mouth. My hips bucked up without my permission, and a growl left his throat as he took a hand and slammed them back down onto the bed.

Motherfucker likes to be in control. Noted.

The way he utterly possessed my body with his mouth was unbelievable. I'd had more blow jobs than I could count, though during the past few I'd really struggled to stay in the moment.

"You taste incredible. Are you feeling okay?" Monroe paused his torture and peered up at me from between my legs, his dark hair falling across his brow line, his lips slick with spit and my precum. Hot. As. Fuck.

"More than okay. God, it feels amazing," I assured him, and my cock twitched in his hand, urging him to do something with it.

"Here's the plan. I'm going to devour this dick until your cum is running down my throat, and after I swallow every last drop, I'm going to shoot my load all over you."

My stomach bottomed out at his filthy words, and he chuckled darkly as he wrapped his mouth around me once again with renewed purpose.

"Monroe, oh god, fuck yes. Suck it just like that," I praised, because fuck, he was talented. One of his hands found my balls and fondled them, which triggered a deep groan from my chest.

"Yeah, make those noises for me, baby. Don't hold back," he demanded as he squeezed my cock tightly.

"Make me come, man. Fuck, yeah." My hips had a mind of their own and lifted off the bed, trying to get deeper. "Oh shit, I'm coming, Monroe. Don't stop. Don't stop."

The most powerful orgasm I'd ever had in my life thundered through my balls and shot out of my pulsing cock with such force that I felt like a goddamned demon had been exorcised from my body.

My cock continued to spurt, and I watched as the sexy bastard between my legs swallowed it all, just like he'd told me he would. His mouth released me with a wet pop, and I moaned when he lapped at the tip of me, taking all evidence of my climax and keeping it for himself.

"Touch me, Kalen." Monroe's husky voice stayed steady, but the dominating tone of it had me moving to obey.

What was it about this guy? If any other person tried to boss me around, I'd fucking deck their ass, and yet here I was, reaching for him. My hand gripped his length and he visibly shivered. He was thicker than I was and his hand covered mine, forcing me to squeeze tighter.

"That's it, Kalen. Fucking squeeze my cock. Yes, like that. Fuck," he hissed.

Monroe was straddling my hips now, our hands twisting and fucking his dick. It was hands down one of the hottest things I'd ever seen. I groaned at the sight, and Monroe leaned down and pressed his lips to mine. Jesus. He devoured my mouth and I was only slightly cognizant of the fact that my hips were grinding underneath him.

"You're so damn sexy," he grunted against my lips, and I smiled into his kiss.

Before I knew what was happening, my other hand was in his hair. "Come for me, Monroe."

"Oh fuck. Fuuuuck," he moaned, moving upright and pumping our hands with vigor. "I'm going to come." His breathing picked up, and the sounds that left his mouth when I felt the first jet of hot cum land on my stomach had my heart skipping a beat.

I squeezed his cock in a pulsing rhythm and he fucking exploded to the finish line. Cum pooled in my belly button as he threw his head back and groaned. Monroe's lithe upper body was dotted with sweat, his chest rapidly rising and falling.

"Jesus," he groaned, flopping over onto his back and staring up at the ceiling.

I had another man's cum in my fucking belly button. I'd come in another man's mouth. And I'd never come so hard in my goddamned life. *Holy shit.*

"You okay over there?" Monroe asked, looking at me from the corner of his eye.

"Me? Yeah, yeah... Of course. I'm just gonna go to the bathroom," I croaked.

"Hold on a sec," Monroe instructed, hopping off the bed and disappearing into the bathroom, returning a few moments later with a damp washcloth.

My face heated up to five thousand degrees as he sat down beside me, still butt ass naked, and wiped his cum from my torso.

"Your abs are a work of art, Kalen. The only thing that makes them look better is my cum all over them. Fuck, what a picture," he breathed and my cock twitched at his attention.

I'd never had someone clean me up after sex. Then again, I usually wasn't covered in fluids like this. My stomach trembled when Monroe trailed his hand down my abs, tracing the definition. I was speechless.

Glancing up to my face, he popped an eyebrow in question. He wanted to make sure I was all right. Was I? Fuck, my head was spinning.

"Thank you," I chuckled nervously. "I'll be back." I sat up, and he moved from the bed so I could stand. I made a beeline for the safety of the bathroom and felt his eyes on my bare ass the entire way.

Closing the door and locking it, I stared at myself in the mirror. Damn, twice in one night now I'd found myself doing this.

Flipping on the warm water, I washed my hands and then my face. It was just sex. We'd both got off.

Had fun. He'd distracted me. That's what I'd needed and was the main reason I'd gone to the bar in the first place. Just because he wasn't a girl didn't mean anything. Right?

I sat on the closed toilet and tried to take some deep breaths with my face in my hands. *Is he going to want to fuck around more? When I get out of here, am I going to let him touch me again?* My dick certainly liked the idea. A fucking lot.

No. Nope. That was a one-off. A one-time thing. I'd never seen Monroe around before, and I highly doubted I'd ever see him again. Nobody would have to know.

But I'd know. The way his tongue had swirled and how he'd swallowed me eagerly. Fuck. I needed to get out of here. I'd already been in the bathroom for at least twenty minutes, hiding out like a wimp.

I'd march out there, grab my clothes, and head home. Flipping the lock, I pulled the door open and shut the light off. My vision took a moment to adjust because there was only a small light on now, and the room was pretty well covered in darkness. I didn't see Monroe immediately, but when my eyes drifted to the massive bed, I saw him lying there with an arm over his stomach, the other above his head.

The man was passed the hell out. His chest was steadily rising and falling as I tiptoed through the room to recover my clothes. Once I slipped them on,

I approached the bed quietly and allowed myself a creeper moment to look at him.

His fair complexion and thick, dark hair were striking, but those damn icy blue eyes under his closed eyelids... They'd been piercing and sharp, just like a glacier. Monroe's dark lashes fanned against his cheeks. He really was... beautiful. Stunning, really. By far the most attractive man I'd ever laid eyes on, and he'd had my cock in his mouth. His lips on mine.

I checked my phone—it was after midnight now. Definitely time to go.

Moving around the bed, I took one last look at him.

"Thank you," I whispered.

What was I thanking him for? I wasn't entirely sure. The distraction? The company? The blow job? Maybe all of the above.

Silently, I let myself out of the room and pressed the button for the elevator. The past week of my life had been a shitshow of epic proportions, and tonight followed the theme. I could only hope that things were going to change. My future was up in the air, but I'd do what I did best. Win.

CHAPTER FOUR

Monroe

The rest of the weekend dragged by slowly after being ghosted by Kalen. The entire night, from the time we ran into each other until the time I fell asleep after the hottest encounter I'd ever had, played on repeat. He'd been so responsive and magnificent, despite his lack of experience with another man.

Magnificent? What the hell was wrong with me? Whatever he was, he'd earned a starring role in my thoughts and fantasies. Now the question was how to track him down without seeming like a fucking stalker. It's not that I wanted a relationship with the guy—I didn't do relationships—I just wanted a follow up session... or twenty.

As I entered the classroom I'd be teaching a summer course in for the next six weeks, I stopped and smiled to myself. I loved teaching bright young minds that were eager to soak up information and hopefully put it to good use in their future careers. Never in a million years had I ever thought I'd want to teach, but all it took was one lecture during my doctorate program, and I was hooked.

Students would be arriving soon, so I made my way to the desk at the front and set up my laptop and papers. Summer session was fast-paced—ten weeks of instruction whittled down to six—but I was ready for it.

Taking a sip of my coffee once I was seated, I pulled up the student directory. Kalen hadn't said outright he was a student here, but I'd bet my left nut he was. The first result for Kalen in the directory was a story from the past week. *Star Catcher Kalen Bishop Shut Out of MLB Draft*. My stomach dropped as I clicked open the link to a picture of Kalen posing for the camera after a game.

Damn. No wonder he'd been having a shitty week. Shaking my head, I closed out of the article and opened up his student profile, noting he was going into his senior year as a communications major.

"Damn it," I muttered. Just my luck—the one time I let my emotions get involved, I couldn't have him.

The last time I'd risked my neck for a man, I'd ended up with a broken heart. I wasn't about to let that happen again for a green-eyed Adonis with an ass that made me want to pursue a Ph.D. in poetry.

Students began coming into the room, and I clicked out of Kalen's profile and pulled up my presentation. Most of them looked tired, which was to be expected at eight in the morning right after a short reprieve from school.

As soon as the clock struck eight, I started class. "Good morning, I'm Monroe Jackson and—" The door opened with a loud squeak, and a baseball hat-wearing punk walked in with AirPods in and his head down. I loudly cleared my throat, and he looked up while taking a bud out of his ear, causing my coffee to threaten to come back up.

Kalen froze in the middle of the aisle and blinked at me with a blank expression before sliding into a seat near the back. *Fucking perfect.* Of course he had to be in my class. How was I going to focus on talking with him sitting right there with his knees spread wide, looking like breakfast?

Straightening my purple tie and smoothing the front of my dress shirt, I regained my composure and finished introducing myself. It took a lot of effort to keep my eyes off of the man in the back of my class, but once I got into my lecture, I let it take over. Two hours passed in a blur and when class was almost over, Kalen was already packed and ready to make a mad dash to the door.

"That's all the time we have for today. Make sure to check your syllabus and submit your response by this evening. Tomorrow, come ready to discuss the reading. Kalen, a word before you leave, please." The room burst into chatter at my dismissal as students began heading out of the room.

I busied myself with packing up my belongings so I wouldn't have to see if Kalen was coming or not. Why did he make me so unsure of myself? My brain wanted to ignore his presence and carry on like he was any other student, but I craved him.

"You wanted to speak with me, *Professor* Jackson?" His voice washed over me like warm rain on a summer's day, and I stopped myself from reacting by slinging my bag over my shoulder to distract myself.

"Yes. Walk with me." My heart thudded in my chest as I walked out of the classroom with him right behind me.

I started walking up the stairs when suddenly I couldn't feel him following me anymore. I stopped at the half landing and looked down at him, still standing a few steps from the bottom.

He adjusted his hat and looked up at me with eyes I wanted to get lost in. His cheeks were pink, and he looked uncomfortable as he shifted his weight from foot to foot.

"Where are we going?" He had returned to being apprehensive and shy. Gone was the man who had let me suck him off and come on his stomach.

"To my office. We need to talk." There was a fifty-fifty chance he was going to follow me.

Turning left at the top of the stairs, I passed several other offices as I pulled my keys out of my bag. My office didn't have a nameplate yet, but that would soon be remedied.

After unlocking my door, I looked over my shoulder. Kalen was just exiting the stairs. I was ecstatic he had followed, but not that it had taken him a few seconds to think it over.

Loosening my tie, I left the door open and walked into the cozy office that was now all mine. There was a great view looking out across a grassy area on campus that in the fall would be alive with students. It was a small room, but had plenty of space for a desk, bookshelves, a loveseat, and two chairs.

"What do we need to talk about?" Kalen walked in and shut the door behind him.

Throwing my bag in a chair, I leaned against my desk, trying to decide the best way to approach the sensitive subject of his dick and mine being acquainted when I was his professor. "Look, Kalen. On a professional level, this can't happen. It's a major conflict of interest."

He held on to the straps of his backpack and nodded. "I don't know what you're talking about."

My eyes narrowed, and I crossed one ankle over the other. "You're going to need to drop my class, because I can't fuck you if you're my student."

His eyes widened and his hands fell to his sides. "What do you mean, I need to drop your class? I just said I didn't know what you were talking about. I'm perfectly fine acting like nothing happened between us."

Fuck. A small pain formed in the pit of my stomach and radiated to my chest. Why did that hurt? I was too young to have a cardiac event over something that was quickly becoming clear he hadn't wanted.

"I'm not fine pretending what happened the other night wasn't the hottest fucking thing I've ever experienced. I shouldn't be teaching any junior or senior level courses this next year, so you can just sign up for this class in the fall." Undoing my tie completely, I stood and took a step toward him.

He shook his head and backed up a step. "I can't drop this class, Monroe. I fucked up spring quarter and if I don't take it now, I'll be on academic probation." He backed into the door as I stopped in front of him. "Which would mean no baseball."

There was no stopping my desire for him. He'd caught me when I was the biggest curveball to head his way. I didn't do relationships or repeated hookups, but we could keep it casual. It was only six weeks, right? How hard could it be to have a clandestine relationship during summer session? Most students weren't on campus or in town, and I had my own place.

"Then I guess we'll have to be discreet." Closing the distance between us, my hands fell to his waist. So much for not putting my neck on the line. "Why'd you leave the other night?"

His head hit the door, and his eyes shut as my thumbs found the skin just above the waistband of his basketball shorts. He was soft and warm against my fingers, and I resisted the urge to drop to my knees and lick him.

"I, uh... well. Fuck." His eyes opened, tumultuous and confused. His jaw locked tight as he shook his head. "I can't."

Licking my lips, I squeezed his waist in an attempt to hold myself back from sliding my hands inside his shorts. "Can't what?" I whispered, angling my head to ghost my lips across his. "We both want this."

A strangled noise came from his throat as I swiped my tongue across the seam of his lips. They tasted like cinnamon, probably from the gum he'd been chewing during class.

My hands slid around to his back, and I pulled

him flush against me as our lips connected. When he'd followed me up the stairs, I hadn't intended for anything to happen besides talking, but I was drawn to him and couldn't stop myself.

His cock hardened against my hip as I probed his lips with my tongue, begging for entrance. He relented, opening for me to sweep inside and taste him. His hand pushed against the back of my neck, molding our mouths together.

"Kalen," I rasped, moving my mouth from his and nipping along his jaw. "I want to bend you over my desk and fuck you so bad right now."

His chest moved with each inhale of breath, and I put my hand there to feel the thudding of his heart as I slipped my other hand into his boxers. His soft skin was hot and slick with his precum. I buried my face in his neck and groaned as I twisted my hand around his shaft.

"I can't do this."

Before my brain even fully processed the blaring warning sirens he had sounded, he pushed me away from him and wiped his mouth with the back of his hand. *Ouch*.

"I think you can. You're just scared. Of what, I don't know." Not trying to hide the effect he had on me, I adjusted myself in my slacks. "Let's start over. Let me take you to dinner."

He was intriguing me more and more each time

he pushed me away. Yes, it hurt to be rejected, but it also lit a fire in me that I hadn't felt in a long time. Now that he'd pushed me away during a hot as hell kiss, all bets were off.

I could tell he wanted me by the blazing inferno in his eyes.

"I'm not scared." He turned to the door, turning the knob but not opening it yet. "It was fun, but it can't happen again, and I'm not going on a date with you." He opened the door and walked out without looking back.

We'll see about that. Kalen Bishop was mine, but if I wanted a shot with him, I would have to do things his way. For now.

CHAPTER FIVE

Kalen

Wiggling my toes in my shoes, I shifted my weight back onto my right leg. *Elbow up, eye on the ball, swing.* Over, and over, and over again. I hadn't achieved a .314 batting average without hours of practice, and there was always room for improvement. So there I was, alone in the baseball training facility, smashing balls right and left in the batting cage.

Batting practice was cathartic for me. I'd practically ran to the training facility with my ass on fire just to get away from Monroe. I felt like I couldn't think properly around him. Misfire on all cylinders. Which was so unlike my personality, and it freaked me the fuck out.

As a catcher, I was always on high alert, watching fucking everything. I had to. A dude steps into the batter box and hits a foul hard down the third baseline? I know he's overeager and chances are he's going to strike out beautifully when I call for a changeup.

Watching the batter's form, paying attention to my pitcher and what calls we're getting from the ump, making sure none of the on-base fuckers get too brave thinking they're going to steal on my ass... I was the eyes of the field, and I fucking lived for it.

Batting though? That was just between me and the ball. Sure, hitting was being on the offensive, moving the players around the bases, but it was calmer than defense. Watching that white ball come flying toward me at high speed, knowing it was going to catch the meaty part of my bat? Yeah, that was the good shit. And right now? It was helping distract me from thinking about *him*.

Professor Monroe fucking Jackson. *My* professor. The man who'd sucked my dick off a few nights ago had just asked me on a damn date. A date!

I still couldn't believe I'd gone up to his hotel room, knowing what was going to happen... and I couldn't stop thinking about it. About him. Then, I'd walked into the first day of my summer school class and there he was, with his piercing blue eyes that stripped me raw right there in the midst of thirty other students.

Jesus, I don't think I retained a damn thing from his entire lecture.

I couldn't go on a date with a man. Though last week, I would've said I'd never let one give me a blow job and then rub his dick with mine, but here we were, and I was fucking confused. Was I bisexual?

Huffing out a laugh, I knocked a ball so hard I wondered if the seams split from the contact. I was destined for Major League Baseball, and being a gay pro athlete—or bi, or whatever the hell—it just wasn't something that happened.

Nobody had to know that I'd fucked around with him. It wasn't like I was going to tell anyone, and that's why I wasn't going to go on a date with the man. We'd probably be seen, and it would be a fucking scandal—one I could *not* afford when I was so close to getting everything I'd worked my entire life to get.

But the way I'd responded to him… Just being near him had my skin tingling and my stomach flipping. I'd never had such an immediate response to a person, and I wasn't sure what to do with that.

The whirring of the machine went on a beat too long, signaling that it needed to be reloaded, so I dropped my bat and stepped back to grab some water.

"Damn, Bishop, nice form. Gotta ask though if you're planning on murdering someone with how hard you were going." Coach chuckled, handing me my water. When the hell had he gotten there?

I pulled off my batting gloves and drank for several seconds before flashing him a classic Kalen smile. "Nah, just perfecting my swing so every pitcher I face next season pisses themselves when I'm on deck." I winked, and Coach barked a laugh.

"Well, I think you're there. Maybe you can show the freshmen a few things next week when they arrive?" he questioned, knowing that I would. I loved helping my teammates improve; it was rewarding as hell.

"You got it, Coach."

"You started your class today, right? Think you're going to be able to keep the grade up?"

Embarrassment burned in my cheeks. I was an absolute beast at baseball—academics, though? Not so much. My previous teachers, my parents, and coaches all said the same shit. 'Kalen, you'd be a 4.0 student if you'd just apply yourself.' Trouble was, I just didn't care enough to do that. There was only one thing I wanted to really apply myself to, and it was baseball.

"Yeah, Coach. Don't worry, I'm going to pass.

Speaking of, I do need to get back to the house and look over the syllabus. We probably have a paper or test soon since it's so condensed," I explained, and he nodded.

"Alright then, Bishop. Proud of you, kid. Keep up the good work. You're gonna have a killer season," he added with a grin and then headed toward his office.

AFTER GRABBING a quick shower and pulling on some shorts, I dropped onto my bed, about to open my laptop and check out the syllabus, when my phone pinged. Rolling onto my back, I tugged it out of my pocket and smiled when I saw the name, Bestie Bitch. She'd put herself in my contacts like that, and the first time I'd seen it—the day after we'd met and exchanged numbers—I knew right then I'd met a friend for the ages.

Bestie Bitch: *Lunch today at Marco's?*

A man needs to eat, right? I could check my school shit later.

Grabbing a clean tank, I threw it on and slipped my feet into some shoes, shooting Nikki a text as the door closed behind me.

Me: *Yeah, meet ya there in fifteen.*

Marco's was a cheap taco truck not far away, and they made the best damn pico de gallo this side of the border. The campus and town were pretty much dead right now since most students returned home for summer break, leaving only those who lived close enough and the athletes who were still training. We were always training, though.

I waved to a few of my teammates on the way out the door. Thankfully, we all got along great, which definitely contributed to how well we played together on the field.

God, it was hot as fuck. Hopping on my bike, I rode the few blocks to Marco's. My back was already sweating, and I wiped my brow. Why did we pick somewhere without air conditioning?

The smell hit me as I locked up my bike, and I remembered why I'd happily sweat to death every damn day if I got to eat this deliciousness.

"Biiiiiitchop!" Nikki shrieked, waving me down from across the street and jumping like a chihuahua. Her messy top knot gave her an extra three inches, but she was only around five-two without it. She had dark brunette hair with some added highlights, a round face, and a smile that brought all the dudes and ladies to their knees, though she was only interested in the latter.

"Must you address me like that in public, you little asshole?" I smirked, pulling her into me for a hug after she skipped across the street.

"Ha. You love when I call you Bitchop. It's funny

because your last name, you know, is Bishop," she snickered, and I rolled my eyes.

"Is it? I had no idea!" I gasped in mock surprise and squeezed her waist, making her spin away from me laughing.

The person in front of us paid for their order and we stepped up, my stomach growling eagerly. We ordered quickly—we were regulars and always got the same thing. Marco made some small talk while he prepared our food, asking each of us about our upcoming seasons.

That was how Nikki and I met. Freshman year, both of us had gotten full-ride scholarships—me for baseball and her for softball. The coaches had thrown a cookout for both teams and the rest was history.

It worked out nicely for her, too. She was a pitcher, and over the past three years, we'd often meet up at the training facility or on an empty field and talk shit while she pitched. I'd give her pointers, which she'd sometimes accept, and other times she'd call me a cocky asshole and try to peg me with a wild pitch.

Marco handed us our orders, and we headed for our usual picnic table that was shaded under a few trees.

"So, how was your communications class? That

was this morning, right?" she asked, taking a huge bite of her shrimp taco.

"Yeah, it was this morning. It was... good. I think," I replied while I examined a chip.

She narrowed her eyes. "You think?"

"What I remember of the class was fine," I told her, scooping some pico and crunching down on the chip. Damn, that was good.

"Are you vaguebooking me on purpose, Kalen? Some of the girls on the team said they saw the new professor. They said he was sent from the heavens. How was he? I'm probably going to have him for something at some point, so lay it on me."

"Seems like an okay guy," I choked out, clearing my throat.

Ever perceptive, Nikki lifted an eyebrow and slowly chewed her food, her eyes narrowing as she studied me. Was my body language screaming 'I'm having a sexual identity crisis?'

"What's going on with you, Kalen Bishop?" Damn, she'd used my whole name.

"Just stressed about this class and my future prospects." Not a complete lie, but not what was currently plaguing my thoughts.

I knew I could confide in Nikki about this—she was gay as gay could be—but I needed to make a little more sense of the situation before I talked to anyone about it.

"Okay then." She shrugged, taking a swig of her water. Well, she'd let that go easier than I'd anticipated. "What are your plans the rest of the afternoon?"

"No clue. I hit the cages already this morning."

"Wanna practice with me? Bea's visiting her mom today so I'm in dire need of a catcher." She winked. Bea was her teammate and the first string catcher, an absolute beast of a player. If I had to go against her in a play at the plate, I'd probably shit myself.

"Works for me, but can we please do it indoors? It's fucking hot, and it's only gonna get hotter," I complained, taking a big bite of my steak taco.

"Aww, little Midwest boy can't take the heat? You should be used to it by now, dude," she teased.

"I'm from Michigan, Northern Michigan. We don't do this level of hell. I'd love to see how your Southern Cali ass handles a foot of snow." We both laughed because I was definitely able to handle this climate better than she'd be able to handle mine in winter.

"I'm going to ignore the fact that you called California Cali." She stood, grabbing our empty plates. "All right, let's get out of here, I wanna work on my riser and curve today. I've been practicing my curveball—you're gonna flip out when you see how hard it breaks!" she squealed, clapping her hands together.

Fuck, I was worn out.

Nikki and I had dicked around at the facility for hours. It was only four in the afternoon, but I needed another shower, and I desperately wanted a catnap.

The house was a ghost town when I got inside, which made me happy because then I could nap in peace. And that's exactly what I did.

Unfortunately, my dreams weren't peaceful. They were of *him*. His hands on my body, his lips on mine, his cock pressed against my ass, his sultry voice telling me to relax, to let him inside. How he was going to fuck me slowly until he filled me up with his cum.

My eyes flew open, and I was panting hard, heart racing. Letting my hand trail down my torso, I shoved it down my shorts and fisted my rock-hard cock. I was pumping myself before I even had time to process.

Hips thrusting, I closed my eyes and pictured myself drilling into Monroe's tight ass, and I detonated moments later, hot cum landing on my stomach and chest. Jesus. What was it about him?

Groaning, I grabbed some tissues off the nightstand and wiped up most of the mess before padding to the bathroom to do a better job.

After cleaning up, I stared at my reflection in the mirror. I looked exactly the same as always, but it felt like I was looking at a completely different person. That night with Monroe had fucked me up, and I didn't know what the hell to do about these things I was feeling.

He was a man. I was a man. How would that even work? The sex was a no-brainer, but what about everything else? I couldn't just start seeing a man.

Weariness over the whole situation made me want to crawl back under my covers and call it a night. Damn, I felt like Rip Van Winkle—what the fuck time of day was it?

I snagged my laptop on the way back into my room, flopping down on the bed just as my stomach growled. Must have been at least dinner time. The screen powered up and I saw it was 7:35 p.m. Damn, I'd slept longer than I'd planned... Oh well, it was summer and it's not like I ever got to sleep in. Between practice and now my summer class, I saw many afternoon naps in my future.

I signed into my student account and accessed Monroe's class, opening the assignments tab. *Shit!* Something was due at eight, which was twenty minutes away.

After reading chapter one of your text, respond to the following using at least two direct quotes from the reading. Your assignment should be APA formatted and will be scored using the following rubric. Late responses will not be accepted.

I skimmed the prompt and stabbed my fingers through my hair, wanting to rip it out.

Motherfucker! How was I going to submit an answer to this question I hadn't even done the reading for? Who the fuck gives an assignment on the first day of class? Had Monroe even talked about it?

Thinking back, I couldn't remember if he had or not because I'd been so fucking distracted by him and the need to hightail it out of there the second class finished.

Damn it, Kalen. You can't fuck this up.

CHAPTER SIX

Monroe

The door shut after the last of my furniture and boxes were carried in by the movers. It had been a long day of teaching, moving into my townhouse, and starting to unpack. I needed a glass of wine and a back massage. Too bad Kalen wasn't around for either of those.

My muscles were so tight, and not just from lifting things to put them where I wanted. I'd gone to grab a quick bite to eat around lunchtime at a delicatessen downtown, and lo and behold, there had been Kalen in all his glory, with a grin bright enough to stop traffic.

But was Kalen alone? Of course not. He was with a cute little pixie who probably climbed him like a tree. She'd darted across the street and practically mounted him as she threw herself into his arms. Shit, was I the other man?

Locating the box with glassware, I carried it to the kitchen island and opened it in search of a wine glass. Deciding I should just unpack the box, I looked around the space to figure out where things should go.

The townhouse was a recent build, so the finishes were modern and new. The living room, kitchen, and dining areas were all open concept. There was a massive white granite island separating the kitchen and dining area from the living room. Dark gray shaker cabinets and chrome accents made it sleek and masculine.

After arranging my drinkware in the cabinet next to the stainless steel refrigerator, I opened one of the cans of wine I'd picked up earlier at the grocery store, pouring myself a glass. I had made the mistake of thinking a can was equivalent to a glass when it was really half a bottle. Never again would I make that mistake.

Soaking in the bath for half an hour relieved most of the tension in my back and hamstrings, and the wine took care of the rest. I rinsed off in the shower and wrapped a towel around my waist before grabbing my laptop and sliding onto a barstool at the island.

My students should have already submitted their first assignments to me, and I was anxious to see what I was working with. As soon as I was logged on, the first email that popped up made my heart speed up.

Kalen Bishop <kalen.bishop@aw.edu>
To: Monroe Jackson <monroe.jackson@aw.edu>
8:06 PM

Professor Jackson,

I am attaching the link to my response since the online portal was down and would not let me submit it.

Thank you,
Kalen Bishop

Pinching the bridge of my nose, I clicked the link, which took me to his document. The assignment had been to write a paragraph written in APA format, with citations based on the assigned reading. With one glance, I could see he had no citations and after reading it, it was clear he hadn't even checked it for errors.

I clicked on the version history and my frown deepened. He'd barely started his assignment at a quarter to eight and last typed on the document a few minutes past the deadline. I wanted to give him the benefit of the doubt and might have, if he'd been honest.

Monroe Jackson <monroe.jackson@aw.edu>
To: Kalen Bishop <kalen.bishop@aw.edu>
8:14 PM

Kalen,

Per the syllabus, responses submitted after 7:59:59 will not be accepted unless there are extenuating circumstances. This information was given in class this morning.

The syllabus also details what was expected in the response, as well as a detailed rubric for grading. Even if the response was submitted on time, it would have received a score of zero as it does not meet the minimum requirements per the rubric.

As a reminder, my office hours are daily, after class, from ten to eleven if you need assistance in reviewing the syllabus or clarification of the rubric expectations.

Monroe Jackson, Ph.D.
Communications Department
Alderwood University

While I waited to see if he was going to respond, I began going through the other responses. During a normal term, I would never have assigned something on the first day, but we had four weeks less and a lot of ground to cover. It was an upper division course too, so I had expected no issues. The other twenty-nine students had all submitted responses on time.

Kalen Bishop <kalen.bishop@aw.edu>
To: Monroe Jackson <monroe.jackson@aw.edu>
8:32 PM

Professor Jackson,

As stated in my first email, the portal would not let me submit my response. I do not think it is fair to be penalized due to a glitch that was out of my control. This class and my grade are very important to me, and not accepting this assignment is unfair.

Kalen

Rolling my eyes at the screen, I reached across the island and poured the rest of the can of wine into my glass. A quad shot of espresso in the morning would cure whatever damage it did.

Monroe Jackson <monroe.jackson@aw.edu>
To: Kalen Bishop <kalen.bishop@aw.edu>
8:41 PM

Kalen,

I understand that your grade and this class are important to you. Of equal importance is prioritizing tasks and meeting deadlines.

As stated in my previous email, the course expectations are explicitly written in the syllabus. Please review it so that you are better prepared for the next assignment.

I also recommend that you not wait until right before assignments are due to begin them. These responses allow me to see if you completed the reading and whether you can apply the material in a meaningful way. It is difficult to score a response that is so clearly rushed.

Please find the attached screenshot of your edit history on the document which shows this was not a technical issue.

Monroe Jackson, Ph.D.
Communications Department
Alderwood University

THERE HAD BEEN NO REPLY to my last email the night before and that really got under my skin. I didn't know what I expected, but an apology of some sort seemed fitting. The frustration added to the slight hangover I had and the soreness still plaguing my back and hamstrings. Why did no one tell me that turning thirty meant pain?

Students began trickling in a few minutes before class started, and every time the door opened, I looked up from my computer screen where I was reviewing what we would discuss during class.

As soon as he entered the room, it felt like all the air had been sucked out. He looked like he'd just rolled out of bed, wearing a wrinkled hooded sweatshirt and a backwards baseball cap with messy brown hair poking through the hole. I wasn't even aware sweatshirts could wrinkle.

He came straight to the front and looked down at me, his green eyes glossy with sleep. "I'd like to submit my response from yesterday." He swung his backpack around, pulled out a paper, and dropped it on my keyboard. "Sorry, it's a little wrinkled in the corner."

I picked it up and glanced at it briefly. "I appreciate the effort, but I can't accept this." It was formatted correctly with clear citations, but it was too little, too late.

"But I—"

I held it out to him and his eyebrows drew together, making a deep line between them. "There will be ample opportunities for you to turn in assignments on time that meet the requirements on the rubric. Please remember this assignment is only worth two percent of your overall grade."

He snatched it out of my hand and shoved it in his backpack in a way that made my stomach flip. I could understand he was upset, but he needed to act like an adult and move on. It was two percent of his grade, for god's sake.

Class felt longer than it should have, and every time I stole a glance at Kalen, he was staring at me with a look that could kill, and it made my entire body tense. By the end of my lecture, my shoulders were burning and my lower back had sharp pains every time I twisted.

"Your next response is due on Friday, and your first midterm is next Tuesday. Please make sure to program these assignments into your calendar. As I stated yesterday and in the syllabus, no late assignments will be accepted." Sucking in a sharp breath of air, I began packing my things, surprised Kalen had left and not come to beg me to accept his assignment again.

I considered canceling my office hours since I was keeling over from pain, but with me being new,

I didn't want to risk looking bad on only the second day.

Instead, I hobbled down the hall to the elevator, since the thought of walking up the stairs made me want to vomit. I'd never judge anyone for using an elevator to go up one level again.

The doors slid open on the second floor and as soon as I was in the hall, I spotted Kalen waiting by my office. Biting my lip, I tried to walk as normally as possible to the door. "Mr. Bishop, I hope you aren't here to throw your paper in my face again."

Opening the door, I stepped in before him, and hastily sat down in my office chair. Kalen gave me a funny look before shutting and locking the door behind him. *What the hell is he doing that for?*

"These are my office hours, Kalen. My door needs to be unlocked." I was curious about what he was doing though.

He dropped his backpack in a chair and grabbed the hem of his hooded sweatshirt. My eyes went wide as he pulled it off, the t-shirt he had underneath riding up and revealing his tight stomach. I wanted to lick each of the indents that made a V right down into his jeans.

To my dismay, he adjusted his shirt after dropping the sweatshirt on top of his bag. "If I was anyone else, you would've given me credit for submitting it."

Trying to process what he had just said, I stared up at him looming over my desk. "What are you suggesting, Kalen?"

He crossed his arms over his muscular chest, his biceps pulling at the sleeves of his dark blue t-shirt. "If I hadn't turned you down yesterday, you would have given me credit."

The urge to fly over the desk and grab him by the throat was hard to resist despite my current state, and I clenched my fists to stop myself. He had some nerve coming into my office and insinuating that my response to him was anything other than professional.

"Get out," I growled between clenched teeth.

"No." Defiance wafted off him like a spell, beckoning me to engage.

Wincing, I stood and put my hands flat on my desk. "I will not allow you to come into my office and intimidate me. So either sit down and discuss your issues like a man or get out."

Maybe I was still drunk from the wine the night before, because the next thing I knew, he was reaching for the button on his pants.

CHAPTER SEVEN

Kalen

What in the actual fuck am I doing?
My fingers deftly worked the button of my jeans, and the sound of my zipper was louder than it should've been within the walls of his office. I could feel my heart pounding in my damn ears.

"Kalen, stop. What the hell is happening right now?" Monroe asked, his face red and pinched with an emotion I couldn't decipher at the moment. Then again, my brain wasn't currently firing on all cylinders.

"I need this grade, okay? Let's just do this, and we can move on. I'm just asking for a fair chance." I reached behind my neck and pulled my shirt off. "I'm going to do the work. I'm not a fuck up, Professor Jackson. I need to take this class, and—"

Monroe slammed his hands down on his desk and winced as though it had caused him physical pain. My mouth closed, and my face flamed with heat. *What the fuck was I thinking?*

"Put. Your. Shirt. On. *Now*!" he barked, and I scooped it up, slipping it on, and then dropped onto the chair in front of his desk.

Oh my god, I'm going to get kicked out of school and baseball will never happen...

"I'm sorry." I exhaled, my eyes fixed on a particularly fascinating design in the wood grain of his desk.

After several torturous minutes—maybe even hours?—I glanced up and found Monroe still leaning with his hands on his desk, staring at me.

"Kalen. As I explained previously, this assignment, in the grand scheme of things, is worth nothing. You weren't prepared for the assignment, you then lied and cited technical difficulties, ignored my explanation completely, waltzed into my class this morning looking like you'd slept for two minutes, and again tried to get me to accept your work." He paused, shaking his head and standing upright with a flinch.

"I know. I'm so sorry, please don't report this," I begged, dropping my face into my hands.

He ignored me.

"And after all that, you come into my office and try to flip this around? That if you'd allowed me to what? *Fuck* you? That you'd be getting an easy A in my class? Is that what you think? I'm so disgusted right now." He shook his head again and rubbed his forehead.

"I'm such an idiot," I mumbled, my leg bouncing with anxiety that needed an outlet.

"Two percent, Kalen. That's the percentage of this assignment toward your overall grade. I know you understand that this is not a make or break thing. So I'm going to ask you, why are you stripping in my office? Because I'm starting to think it has nothing to do with the assignment, and more of you trying to give yourself an excuse to make this acceptable between us.

"You want to fuck around? Fine. I already told you I wanted that, but I don't play games. I'm openly gay, I have nothing to hide, and I'm not ashamed of my sexuality. I had a great time with you the other night, but this is your one and only warning. Do not ever question my ability to be a professional, do you understand?"

Fuck. Sweat was running down my spine, and I was so embarrassed at my behavior, I wished the floor would crack open and just swallow me whole.

"I'm sorry. I don't know what the fuck is wrong

with me. Everything is so messed up. I was supposed to be drafted, and here I am for another year. A year I wasn't planning on, and I fucked my grades up last semester. My dad is on my ass and threatening to cut me off. I don't even know what I'd do without baseball. It's only ever been baseball!" I slammed my hands on the armrests and stood up, running my hands through my hair. My dad was going to kill me.

"Hey," Monroe said softly, like he was addressing a wild animal. I sure fucking felt like one.

I dropped my hands to my sides and stared at him, my face so hot I was sure it was on fire.

"You've got a lot going on. I understand that, but when it comes to this class, if you need help with anything, just let me know. It's clear you're passionate about your sport. That's admirable. Let me look over your paper. I'm still not accepting it, but I can let you know my thoughts, which might help for future assignments," Monroe offered, sitting down with a wince that reminded me of how I acted the day after a hard workout.

"Thank you, I appreciate it," I told him genuinely.

Fuck, I was a fool. The guy was a total professional, and I'd just completely offended him. While I worked on getting my paper from my bag, Monroe shifted uncomfortably in his seat.

"You okay?" I asked, lifting an eyebrow as I slid the assignment across his desk.

He grunted, reaching for my paper. "Yeah. Movers moved everything into my place yesterday, but I had to do a lot of heavy lifting. Overdid it. Pulled a muscle in my back and my hamstrings have been screaming all day," he explained, scanning my work.

"Hamstring pain is the work of the devil; no one can convince me otherwise," I told him seriously. I'd pulled one back in high school and my athletic trainer had my ass in so many ice baths I'd practically turned into a walking snowman. "So? What do you think?" I questioned, referring to my assignment.

Monroe laid the document down and shrugged. "Well, it's... okay. I probably would give it a C at best."

My mouth fell open. "A C? Are you serious? That took me three hours to complete."

His eyebrows lifted. "Three hours? Kalen, this should take an hour, an hour and a half at most. That's why it was a first day assignment—short and sweet."

My face flamed. Great. Now he was going to think I was an idiot. Just a meathead jock.

"I'm really fucking stressed. I feel like I can't concentrate on anything and I just space out. I'm really freaking out. I can't fail your class, Monroe," I bit out, eyes on the floor.

"I think you need a friend." My eyes snapped to

his. "I need a friend too. I don't know anyone here. I'm willing to help you get your head on straight and make sure you stay focused on completing your assignments in a reasonable amount of time. There's an assignment due on Friday. How about you come by my place tomorrow and you can work on it while I work on preparing my lectures?"

I studied him. Was he really just wanting a friend? The image of him sucking my dick popped into my head and a generous amount of blood headed south. I wasn't gay... right?

"Just friends?" I asked.

Monroe laughed deeply and shook his head at my question.

"Yes. Just friends. My ego can only handle being turned down so many times. Let's get you sorted out so you can meet your academic goals. I'll be your focus buddy in exchange for you telling me everything I need to know about this town. Best food places, shops, bars. Deal?" He smiled and his blue eyes twinkled.

With the pressure off regarding whatever chemistry there was between us, I felt like he'd actually be someone I'd like to get to know better. As a friend. Strictly platonic.

"Deal. Thank you so much for this. You won't regret it," I promised, standing and reaching for a sticky note and pen from his desk. "Here's my number." I scribbled it down and handed it to him. "Just let me know where I'm meeting you tomorrow."

"Sounds good. Bring your laptop and your book, and be prepared to study," he said firmly.

I reached for the door handle, but spun back. "Please forgive—"

Monroe held his hand up, cutting me off. "Get out of here, Kalen. See you tomorrow." He smirked, turning his attention to his laptop, and I slipped into the hallway.

Holy shit. Adrenaline was pumping through my veins, and I raced out of the building. I needed to smash some baseballs.

CHAPTER EIGHT

Monroe

Glancing around my living room, I took in the mess of boxes and furniture that I had yet to move or unpack. It wasn't that I didn't want to get my house in order, but I'd been resting my back.

Today, though, I felt like a million bucks. Not to mention Kalen was coming over, and I couldn't have him seeing this mess.

What had happened in my office the day before was unbelievable. It was a cry for help, and I couldn't ignore it. There were strict guidelines about how close faculty could be with students in their department, and I was walking the line. I wouldn't be able to help him with preparing his assignments, but I could certainly keep him from zoning out or spending time scrolling on his phone.

I still couldn't believe he'd agreed to come over to my house, but no complaints here.

You're just friends, idiot. If I said it enough times, I'd start to believe it, right? Kalen was in no place to be anything other than friends, especially since I'd seen him with that girl, and he was already on edge about what we'd done together.

After moving a few boxes to the correct rooms, the pain in my back started again, and I lay down on the couch, seeking relief. I'd at least managed to clear off the couch and coffee table so we could have a work area.

Pulling out my phone, I swiped open my messages and smiled at the texts from Kalen. He'd given me his number, and I'd texted him my address. So far, that was the only conversation we'd had. That was the only conversation we *should* have.

Kalen: *Want me to bring dinner later? I was thinking pizza sounded good, but if you want something else...?*

Monroe: *Bring your A game with the pizza. I make the best.*

Kalen: *Sure you do... There's this bomb place that's the best around. What toppings do you want?*

Monroe: *We'll see how bomb it is. There's not much I don't like, so get whatever toppings.*

Did I get a few butterflies in my stomach thinking about him bringing dinner? Yes. Was I proud of that fact? Jury was still out on that. *Just friends.*

His office freak-out left me confused and intrigued by him. He was under a lot of pressure from home, which I had a hard time wrapping my head around. How could a father be so overbearing and unsympathetic to the demands of a college athlete vying for a spot on a professional team?

My own family was nothing but supportive of not only my career, but my sexuality as well. It might have felt embarrassing as hell to have your parents accompany you to a Gay Pride parade at fourteen with rainbow flags and glittered hair, but I was glad I had their support.

I must have fallen asleep for several hours because the shrill sound of my doorbell pulled me out of a dream I probably shouldn't have been having about Kalen. People had sex dreams about their friends all the time, didn't they?

I rolled off the couch, using the coffee table to help me stand. My back was so fucked and to make matters worse, my dick was hard as a rock. I was doing a really good job of putting my desire aside.

While I adjusted myself, I shuffled to the door and attempted to not look like the Hunchback of Notre Dame. The smell of pizza drifted in as I opened the door. "Hey there." Biting my lip, I kept off the *baby* I wanted to tack on to my greeting.

"Hey." He gave me a funny look and looked past me into my house. "Are you going to invite me in?"

Did he know he was doing and saying the exact same thing he had the night we'd hooked up?

"Come on in." *Snap out of it, Jackson, he's here as a student and brought you dinner as a thank you.* I moved to the side so he could enter, and shut the door behind him. "We can eat at the island or in the living room. Wherever you're comfortable. Do you want something to drink?"

"Water would be great." He headed to the couch, and I went to the kitchen to fill two glasses with water. Swallowing my pride, I also grabbed an ice pack from the freezer.

"I got pepperoni and sausage." He already had the lid open and was serving up slices on paper plates that had come from the pizza place. "What's wrong?"

"Hm?" I was still standing, wondering how the hell I was going to put the drinks down and sit without bending. "Here, take the waters."

After handing them off, I sat down like I was nine months pregnant and put the ice pack against my back. Concern filled his eyes, and I waved him off.

"Have you been taking it easy? If you strained your muscles, you should be resting." He handed me my plate and started eating his slice of pizza.

"I may have moved a few boxes..." He raised an eyebrow. "And taken an extra long nap on the couch."

"After your back feels better, maybe you need some strength training. How old are you?" He had already demolished an entire slice and leaned forward to grab a second. "Wait, let me guess. You're like Doogie Howser and were a child prodigy. Twenty-four? You look hella young to be a professor."

Barking out a laugh, I picked a piece of sausage off and ate it before answering. "You're a little young to know who Doogie is."

"My mom made us watch it growing up. She said she wanted one of her kids to be a doctor." He shrugged, and I swear he shoved half a slice in his mouth in one go. Jesus, that was a mental image I needed to get out of my brain. Friends. We were *friends.*

Friends that had partaken in some fun times in a hotel room. And damn, if I didn't want to do more with the man sitting next to me, but maybe once he got his act together. "I'm thirty. Did your mom get her wishes fulfilled?"

"Nope." He popped the p and sighed. "My oldest sister was pregnant at sixteen and my middle sister probably does porn."

I nearly choked on my bite of pizza. Coughing, I

did a grabby hand motion toward my water, because the thought of leaning forward to get it made me want to cry. He handed it to me with a grin. He was lying.

"No really, though. My older sister really did get pregnant at sixteen. And Audrey... well, she's a free spirit who sells handmade carved soaps on Etsy. Apparently, she makes a lot of money." He shrugged and nodded to the pizza box. "Ready for another slice? Isn't it amazing?"

"Sure, and it's okay. I make way better pizza than this." God, that sounded cockier than I wanted it to, but I really did make excellent pizza.

"Well, now I'm curious because *this* is the best pizza on the West coast." Kalen put another slice on my plate. "Once you're all moved in, you should let me judge your pizza for myself."

"I reserve my culinary skills for special people only." Smirking, I took a big bite of pizza. It wasn't bad pizza, but it wasn't mine.

"Are you saying I'm not special?" He winked, and I damn near choked again. For wanting to be friends, he was certainly laying on the charm.

Shrugging, I didn't respond at first because we were headed down a slippery slope to full-on flirting. He was confused, to say the least, and I didn't want to contribute to that confusion any more than I already had. Which meant I probably shouldn't have invited him over, but no one's perfect.

"Uh... we should finish up, so you can get started on your assignment." The best thing to do was ignore what I really wanted to say and do. He appeared to be more comfortable around me now and that was both a blessing and a curse.

After Kalen completed his assignment—which only took an hour since I took his phone away and suggested he take notes—he packed up his laptop and book before standing and swinging his bag over his shoulder.

"Thanks for your help. Taking notes while reading definitely helps. Makes me wonder how well I could have done all these years." He looked around the living room as I pushed myself up off the couch. "Do you need help moving stuff?"

"It can wait until my back is better." Wincing, I leaned over to grab the two empty glasses off the coffee table. "My long run tomorrow might help."

"Your long run? Dude, you're going to make it worse." He dropped his bag on the couch and took the glasses from me. "Take it easy for a few days."

He was right, I knew he was, but I was also a bit stubborn when it came to my routines. I'd already missed two short runs, and the half marathon I'd signed up for at the end of July wasn't going away.

Grumbling to myself, I stood there helpless as he cleaned up. "I thought you were supposed to stay active during an injury."

"Yeah, but running? That's high impact. What's your strength training like?" He picked up his bag again and looked me up and down, as if assessing my muscles.

"Push-ups, sit-ups, and pull-ups when I think about it." I walked him to the door. "I do some hill work too, especially if I'm training to run on a hilly course."

Kalen stopped just outside the door and braced himself with his hands on the door frame, looking back at me. The position made his arm muscles appear huge in his t-shirt.

"How about I come over tomorrow to move stuff for you, and we can talk more about your lack of a strength training program?"

"You really don't have to do that, Kalen." The more he was around, the harder it was going to be for me to stick to being only friends.

I was inexplicably drawn to him. Outside the classroom or my office, my brain seemed to completely ignore the minor detail of him being my student and the incredibly inappropriate striptease he'd performed in my office just the day before.

"That's what friends do, right? Help each other out. You help me, I help you." Why did it feel like he was insinuating something else? I really needed to get my mind out of the gutter. "I'll see you in class tomorrow, Professor Jackson."

With a grin, he left me standing at the door wondering what the hell I was doing being *just friends* with a man who made me weak in the knees.

CHAPTER NINE

Kalen

With renewed confidence, I found myself sitting in Monroe's classroom the next morning. He'd really helped remind me of what good study habits were, which I'd known but just hadn't cared to use.

Last night at his house had been fun. A lot of fun. He was easy to talk to, we laughed, and he even joked with me a little. He always carried himself with this air of seriousness and intensity, so it was refreshing to see the guy actually break a smile and laugh out loud.

I was a little surprised that he'd seemingly backed off in his pursuit of me. He seemed to be taking the friends thing seriously, so maybe that was why I felt a weight had been lifted from my shoulders.

With everything going on in my life—baseball, my dad, my future, the list went on and on—questioning my sexuality was likely the thing to send me spiraling over the edge headfirst into a mental breakdown of epic proportions.

With Monroe stepping back, it made it possible for my head to clear a bit. Not to say I wasn't still confused. Because *fuck*. I'd fucked around with a man, and if I was being totally honest, I wanted to do it again. Not just any man, though. Only Monroe.

Giving myself mental whiplash was clearly something I'd get an A in if it was a graded subject.

I was jolted from my thoughts when people started standing and heading for the door. I glanced down at my watch and saw that class was over. It had flown by faster than usual.

"Bishop, you heading for the cages?" Williams asked, clapping his hand on my shoulder in passing.

"Yeah, dude. I'll be there in about ten minutes. See ya soon."

Damn, I hoped I hadn't missed anything important in the last five minutes of class. I'd done so well staying focused during the lecture. I guess Rome wasn't built in a day.

I shoved my laptop into my backpack and was about to stand when I sensed someone standing next to me. Well… smelled someone. His scent invaded my space and it made my head swim. He smelled like a forest and pure, unadulterated man.

"What'd you think of the lecture?" Monroe asked, loosening his tie and running his hand down the length of it like it *wasn't* a tie.

I tilted my head back a bit to look up at him. He was dressed in gray slacks with a pale blue dress shirt that he'd rolled to his elbows. His tie was a floral pattern with pale pink and blue flowers and vibrant green vines and leaves. It looked damn good on him. *Wonder what it would look like against my wrists...*

I mentally bitch-slapped myself, then my cock for good measure.

Trying to get a hold of myself, I cleared my throat. "It was good. Thanks for reminding me that notes are my new best friend—it was really beneficial today. Amazing how something so simple can be forgotten." *No, Kalen, you've just been a lazy fuck.*

He squinted his eyes, studying my face, and I swallowed. *Why is he so intense?* Something flashed over his expression, and then he stepped back.

"Great. Well, I'll see you later?" he asked, lifting a dark brow.

What the fuck is that all about?

"Yeah, for sure. Just let me know what time. Gotta head to the cages, batting practice," I explained, finally standing and swinging my bag around to my back.

"Oh, yeah, sorry. Didn't mean to delay you. See you later then." Monroe smiled, but it didn't meet his eyes.

Maybe he doesn't want me to help move his shit around? Then he turned to walk away and that fake smile turned into a real grimace, and I knew the guy was still hurting.

"Careful with that back, old man," I taunted, and he glowered at me.

"Watch your smart mouth, baby," he fired back without missing a beat.

He did not just call me baby. Well, he did, but not like his baby. *He meant an infant. A human infant child baby. A tiny, screaming baby.*

My dick didn't buy it. I needed to get out of there before he saw my erection through my damn basketball shorts. Why was this so awkward?

"Bye, Mr. Bishop." Monroe smirked, turning gingerly and walking away from me.

After spending the rest of the morning practicing with a few of the guys, I went home and hopped in the shower.

It was ridiculous. Absolutely ridiculous. *I'm attracted to Monroe.*

There was no point in denying how I felt any longer. I was, at the very least, bisexual. I'd slept with tons of women and had a great time doing so... or that's what I'd thought. Then, I'd had some third base sex with Monroe, and it was literally the hottest fucking thing I'd ever experienced. All of my past sexual encounters paled in comparison.

Monroe was sexy, confident, and he wanted me. Badly.

My hand found my hard dick, and before I knew it, I was pumping furiously, thinking about all the things I wanted him to do. Shit, the man had sucked my cock like he wanted to pull it from my body. *I wonder what he'd taste like...*

I thought about how he'd run his hand down his tie earlier, like it was me he was stroking. You couldn't tell me he didn't know what he was doing. Fuck, I wanted his hands on me again. His mouth, his tongue.

My balls tightened and I came with a growl, shooting my cum all over the shower wall.

Twice in one week, I'd touched myself thinking of a man. When we messed around at the hotel, I was drunk. The day after? Confused as hell. But the attraction was not only there while sober, it was getting stronger every single time I was near him.

I toweled off, and my stomach flipped in anticipation of going to his place again tonight.

It was just after seven when I got to Monroe's. Since it was so late in the day, I'd stopped and grabbed a couple pints of ice cream for later. I smoothed my hands down my skintight black t-shirt that went well with my gray sweat shorts. Chicks always commented on this outfit so I figured Monroe might also appreciate it. And I realized I *wanted* him to notice me.

Monroe called out for me to come in when I knocked, so I swung the door open and found him lying on the couch.

"How ya feelin'?" I asked, walking straight to the freezer to dump the ice cream in before it melted.

"A little better today, but I think it's just sore now because I've been moving around a lot. What are you doing?" he questioned, sitting up and watching me rummage in the freezer.

"Oh, I brought ice cream for later," I explained with a shrug as I moved over to where he was sitting. His eyes tracked me the entire time, and it made my heart race.

"Ah... a man who likes dessert, huh?" he teased, popping a dark brow.

I grinned, looking down at him. "Well, I figured I might get hot with all this physical labor and I brought the best ice cream this side of the North Pole."

"Is that so? I might get hot by association. Good thinking on the ice cream," he bantered.

Looking around the room, there were still several boxes that needed unpacking, a large bookshelf that was empty, furniture that needed rearranging, and who knew what else.

"So, where do you want me to start?" I asked, walking around the living room and taking inventory.

"Let's start with this room." Monroe pushed himself up off the couch and walked over to the bookshelf.

"All right, boss me around. I'm at your service this evening," I flirted, and he knew it by the way his head snapped in my direction, those blue eyes locking on me.

"You asked for it, just remember that."

THREE HOURS LATER, I was sweating and ready for a break, but everything was in its right place. Monroe had tried several times to get involved with the lifting, and I'd scolded him each time. He grew more and more frustrated at not being able to help, but that's what he got for trying to be Superman and move in completely on his own.

We'd flirted and laughed the entire time. If clothes could be removed from heated stares, I would've been butt ass naked after the first two minutes. You could have cut the sexual tension with a knife.

I felt a little guilty because the man was trying so hard to keep his hands to himself. A few times, he'd reached out to touch me and dropped his hand so quick it was like a cinder block was tied to it. I knew it was because of my asshole behavior earlier in the week. I appreciated it, though.

My ass hit the couch, and I groaned with relief.

"Water, wine, or beer?" Monroe offered.

"Beer sounds amazing. Thanks," I replied.

A moment later, he handed me an ice cold bottle and then lowered himself onto the other end of the couch, effectively putting some distance between us. I didn't comment, instead, drinking half the bottle in one go.

Monroe licked his lips and lifted his canned wine to take a drink. Yeah, *canned* wine. I'd never seen that shit in Michigan or anywhere before.

"How did you know you were gay?" I blurted out, causing him to nearly inhale his drink.

"Fuck, Kalen, you've got to stop choking me like that," he cursed.

Did I though? Maybe he would like me taking him from behind, my hands around his neck...

"Sorry..." I muttered.

He cleared his throat. "I knew I was gay when I was eight. I developed a major crush on one of my friends, and as the years passed, I never felt that way toward any of the girls I was around. I came out at thirteen to my parents, and they were very supportive," he explained.

"Wow. That's... awesome. About your parents, I mean," I clarified, taking another sip of my drink.

"I was lucky. Not everyone is, unfortunately." Monroe shook his head, and I blushed because I was thinking about how my own father would react if he found out about what I'd done with Monroe. What I wanted to continue doing with Monroe…

I cleared my throat. "Yeah, I bet."

"Kalen? You mentioned your dad the other day in my office. What's the deal there? Not a good relationship?" he speculated, taking a sip of his wine.

An unattractive snort left my nose. "You could say that. My dad used to play ball. He never made it to the majors. Ended up tearing his ACL when he rounded a base wrong, and he never fully recovered from it.

"He's always been very strict. Not just with me,

but also with my sisters. You remember how they turned out. I feel a shitload of pressure from him to basically not be a fuck up. I'm the only child he has left who might not embarrass the shit out of him. Not that my sisters are an embarrassment. I love them, but to him, I'm his last chance at greatness," I explained.

"That's a lot to put on your shoulders," he commiserated, and I shrugged.

"It is what it is, man. I do love the game. I'm fucking good at it. When I'm on the field, I'm the one who has eyes on everything. I'm the only player who can see it all, so I'm the most vocal. The guy who screams and directs where the ball needs to go. It's a fuckin' rush. When I step into the dirt and lower my mask, I come alive. There's never been another feeling in my life that's come close to that." Aside from being with him.

Monroe nodded. "I understand that. When you find something that makes your heart pound and your adrenaline pump, you don't let it go." His eyes were burning me alive. He stood and shook his empty can, signaling the need for another.

As he passed by me, I replayed those words. He was right. Fuck all this shit.

My feet were carrying me to the kitchen before I was even aware of it. The fridge was open and Monroe was leaning down to get us new drinks, the fabric of his flamingo printed white shorts pulling taut against his ass.

The moment he spun around, I was right there. Chest to chest.

"Kalen," he gasped, surprise evident on his face. His eyes searched mine, and his pupils dilated. My dick was so hard I felt like I could use it as a hammer if he needed some art hung up.

Stepping closer, our bodies pressed together and heat exploded down my spine. *Fuuuuuck.* I lifted my hand to his face, trailing my fingers across his jaw until I made it to his mouth. My thumb slid across his pouty bottom lip, and his warm breath on my skin had my eyes fluttering.

"You said when you find something that makes your heart pound, to not let go. Well, I found it." Grabbing the back of his neck and pulling him toward me, I took his mouth in a brutal kiss that made my knees go weak.

Monroe groaned and I heard the thud of the can hitting the kitchen floor. A second later, his arms were wrapped around my waist, and his erection was firmly against mine. Damn, he felt so good.

Our tongues were battling, and all I could think about was needing more. No sooner had the thought entered my mind than Monroe's hand was fisting my hair and tilting my head back, exposing my throat. The loss of his mouth on mine had me whimpering.

"Are you fucking with me, Kalen?" Monroe's voice rumbled, causing goosebumps to explode from my skin.

"No, I wouldn't do that to you," I told him honestly.

He ran his tongue from the base of my neck up to my ear, and holy shit, my brain was short-circuiting. *What is it about this man?*

"I don't play games. From the minute I saw you, I wanted you. Tell me what you want, Kalen," Monroe purred, his breath warm against my ear.

Reaching up, I took his hand from my hair and put it on my chest. Our faces were barely an inch apart now.

"You asked me out, on a date. When I turned you down, you said I was afraid. I was... no, I *am* fucking terrified, Monroe. Do you feel my heart right now? Nobody has ever caused such a physical reaction until you. So what do I want?" I growled, backing him up against the counter.

My hand snaked between our bodies, and his eyes flared when I palmed his solid cock. Jesus, it felt like steel. "I fucking want you, Monroe. I can't take it anymore. Fuck. I just... I have to know what this is between us. You make me feel alive," I confessed.

"Thank god, I don't think my balls could take

another day of not having you. Good thing you set up my room," Monroe chuckled, like the sex god he was. His hand slipped into mine, and he pulled me behind him to the bedroom, the can of wine left abandoned on the floor.

My stomach flipped in anticipation of what we might do, but I didn't have long to think about it because the moment I stepped through the doorway, his lips were on mine again. It was rough and possessive, like he was trying to stamp himself on my soul.

I felt my shirt lifting, and we broke the kiss momentarily, just long enough to get the thing off and tossed aside. Monroe groaned when his hands hit my bare skin.

"Less clothes," I panted, helping him out of his shirt. "I need to feel your skin on mine."

We helped one another strip down, which probably took longer than necessary because we couldn't keep our hands or lips to ourselves.

"Fuck, baby. You're a work of art," Monroe praised, stepping back to stare at me unabashedly.

"If you don't get your hands on me in the next two seconds, I'm going to explode, and then you'll have nothing pretty left to look at," I taunted. I'd been shy and timid the first time we were together, but that's not how I usually was.

Monroe tossed his head back and laughed deeply, before piercing me with those intense eyes.

"Get on the bed, Kalen," he ordered.

I practically strutted my naked ass to his bed, climbing up and sitting so my back was near the headboard.

"What do you want to do?" Monroe asked, stroking himself slowly while his eyes trailed all over my body.

"I just want to do what feels right. I'll let you know if something doesn't. Get over here, Monroe," I gritted out, fisting my own cock now. God, I needed him to make me detonate.

He prowled over to the bed, crawling up to me. The glint in his eyes revealed how much he was loving this.

"Unfortunately, I won't be able to fuck you tonight..." He trailed off, urging me to lay down. "Not how I'd want to, anyway."

"Shut the fuck up and kiss me," I demanded, tugging him up by his shoulders.

"You're not as shy as I remembered, Kalen," Monroe chuckled, but that was cut short when I flipped us so he was flat on his back and I was hovering above him, my arms supporting my weight.

I dipped my face down and licked his lips. His tongue flicked out and teased mine. Such a simple act, but it was incredibly erotic.

Monroe let me slip between his thighs, his hands gripping my ass in encouragement, and I slid my cock against his. Our grunts and groans of pleasure were a heady fucking combination that just amped up the desire consuming my body.

"You feel better than I remember," I admitted, kissing his neck and nipping lightly with my teeth.

"Been thinking about me a lot, baby?" Monroe taunted.

"Fuck, you have no idea..." My hand gripped his dick. I moved it in the same way I liked to handle myself and that seemed to be the right thing to do, judging from the sounds he was making.

"Did you touch yourself and think about me this week? Tell me the truth," Monroe growled as he wrapped his hand around mine, taking control of the motions.

"Yes. Twice. When I wasn't doing that, I was thinking about it. You drive me crazy."

"I need to feel your mouth, Kalen. Are you ready for that?" Monroe asked, and my heart warmed. Even the first time we hooked up, he'd been concerned about me being comfortable.

"God, yes. I want to make you feel good," I confessed, sitting back on my heels to get a better view of him.

"Feeling is mutual. Climb up here and turn

around, I want to taste you too," he said, crooking his finger and beckoning me to obey.

I'd never been the person on top during a sixty-nine, but there was a first time for everything. The moment I swung my leg over his face, my balls were sucked into his mouth, and I almost shot my load in surprise.

"Fuuuck," I swore.

Bending over him, I gripped his cock and tentatively licked the tip. That earned me a twitch. When I licked him again, flattening my tongue, his dick jerked and the moan that he unleashed reverberated around my balls. *Jesus Christ.*

I wrapped my lips around him and again, just went off of what I enjoyed when I got a blow job. My head moved up and down, my fist twisted and squeezed, and my other hand massaged his balls. I could barely fucking focus with the way he was sucking on me.

His tongue moved from my sack to my taint, and I almost choked.

"Let me lick you, baby. I'm going to make you feel so good," he promised, and I resumed my work on him.

My heart was racing in anticipation. His hands spread my cheeks and he ran his tongue from the base of my dick all the way back to my ass. Oh. My.

God. Nobody had ever done that to me before, and it was fucking amazing.

I worked his cock harder, taking him deeper and in turn, he ate me like a starved man. My hips began to grind and his fingers sank into my skin. Monroe pulled back and groaned loudly when I took him to the back of my throat.

"Shit, Kalen. I'm going to come."

"Yeah," I grunted. "Come for me, Monroe."

He licked my ass again before moving back to my balls, and just as I was deep throating him, I felt his finger press against my tight hole. Monroe applied gentle pressure and moved in circular motions and I couldn't help it. I'd never felt anything like that.

"Oh god! Monroe, fuck. Yes. I'm coming. I'm coming," I chanted, rocking my hips and pumping my hand on his cock in sync with my hips. My orgasm hit me like a wrecking ball against a brick wall. Absolutely fucking explosive. Leaning down, I wrapped my lips around him again and groaned in encouragement when he began lifting his own hips, fucking my mouth.

He came with a roar and a slap to my ass, his hot cum shooting to the back of my throat, the taste of him was slightly salty with a sweetness that I hadn't expected. I swallowed it down eagerly.

I made him come in my mouth. And I fucking loved it.

Moving off him, I collapsed so I was beside him

on the pillow. We were both sweating and panting, thoroughly satisfied.

"You suck cock like a pro," Monroe praised, chuckling.

"Well, I don't do anything half-assed," I quipped, grinning at him.

He rolled over and propped himself up on his elbow, tracing a circle on my pec. "So, we're going to do this?"

I covered his hand with mine, shocked that it felt so natural to hold his hand to my chest in such an intimate way. "I don't know what the fuck I'm doing, but yeah. What do we have to lose?"

Everything. I had everything to lose.

CHAPTER TEN

Monroe

Staring at the man next to me as he snored softly, I couldn't believe he'd spent the night in my bed. I rolled onto my back and stared at the ceiling. I wasn't sure what we were doing or where it was headed, but I needed to be careful.

I barely knew the man, and he was already constantly on my mind. I hadn't felt so strongly for someone since... well, ever. Even with my ex, I hadn't been this enamored.

Slipping out of bed, I was as quiet as possible, escaping to the bathroom to take care of business and brush my teeth. He had looked so peaceful, and I didn't want to wake him. It was only seven and there were no classes on Fridays, so he'd probably want to sleep in.

After pulling on some shorts, I padded out to the kitchen to start my day. Coffee. Emails. Drawing. Before I started my coffee maker, I picked up the can of wine I'd dropped the night before when Kalen had kissed me like I was the last person on Earth. I could still feel him on my lips and the feel of his stubble between my legs.

Jesus, I sounded pathetic.

I put the wine back in the refrigerator and checked my messages while I waited for my coffee to brew. Maybe if I kept myself busy, my mind wouldn't wander to the erotic scene from the night before.

My phone vibrated with a text as I read and responded to a few emails, and I smiled. My sister texted almost every morning. She'd been doing it since I moved away for college over a decade ago.

Marilyn: *Hey, shithead, hope you have a great Friday. Why did you move so far away?*

Me: *I'm literally two hours away.*

Marilyn: *That's too far.*

Me: *I could always move back to Chicago.*

Marilyn: *You wouldn't! Don't ruin my Friday with your idle threats.*

Me: *Come visit me... Oh, and I met someone...*

The phone rang and I quickly rejected her call.

She would pepper me with a million questions I probably didn't have the answers to. Her squealing might even wake up Kalen.

Me: *Not now. He's sleeping still.*

Marilyn: *OMG, he slept over! I need all the details, right now. About him, not what you did with him.*

Me: *It's new. He's younger. My coffee is ready! Have a great day!*

Marilyn: *Asshole.*

Yeah, it was probably a mistake telling her, but I couldn't resist. Smiling to myself, I poured a cup of coffee and got comfortable on the couch with my sketchbook.

I'd started drawing and painting in high school after taking an art class, and hadn't stopped since. I didn't do it as much as I used to, but still enjoyed the stress relief it brought me. Plus, I'd made some extra money by turning the sketches into paintings.

I was just starting my second sketch when the bedroom door opened and Kalen emerged. He might as well have been walking out naked instead of just in his dark blue boxer briefs. He shuffled over to the kitchen, grabbed a glass, and filled it with water.

My eyes took in his wide shoulders, narrow waist, and ass that deserved its own shrine. His body was a work of art, a true testament to his devotion to baseball. He'd spent years building his muscles to perform at their best, and last night, I'd had my hands all over them.

"Morning," he mumbled around the rim of his glass as he turned and leaned against the counter. If I hadn't already been awake, the view of him from the front would have woken me right up. I didn't know if I liked the view of the back or the front more.

Who was I kidding? Definitely the front.

"Hi." My eyes traveled down his body from where his Adam's apple bobbed as he drank water, to his defined pecs with dusky nipples, his chiseled abs, and the bulge in the front of his boxers.

He set the glass on the counter and walked toward me, his quads flexing and his boxers pulling even tighter across his thighs. I needed to roll my tongue up before it collected dust off the floor. He sat down next to me on the couch, his leg pressing against mine and his arm going to the back of the couch. "What are you up to?"

Thinking about how I want to lick you from head to toe. "Just doodling."

He examined the outline of the flower I was sketching. "That's no doodle. Can I see your book?"

Biting my lip, I handed it over. "There's nothing special about it. Some I turn into paintings." There was something intimate about showing him my sketches. There were a few non-floral sketches but the majority of them were just flowers.

He flipped through a few pages and then held the book up, laughing. That wasn't a good sign. Not a good sign at all. "Dude. I thought you were gay."

"What?" I snatched the book back and frowned at the flower he had been laughing at. "What does me drawing flowers have to do with my gayness?"

He pointed to a petal. "Those, my friend, are pussies."

It felt like the thermostat had been turned up to one hundred. "They are not. What are you even talking about?"

"Let me have your phone." I unlocked my phone and handed it to him. Shit, maybe I shouldn't have in case my sister decided to text me something inappropriate. He opened the browser and typed something in and then handed it back. "Maybe your subconscious is telling you that you like pussy."

"Oh my god. Stop." I dropped the phone on my sketchbook and covered my face. It was fucking embarrassing that I hadn't even realized I was drawing petals which looked like female anatomy. "No wonder people pay up to five hundred dollars when I paint these."

"Are you blushing?" He grabbed one of my arms and pulled my hand away from my face. "You are!" He leaned over and kissed my cheek, causing both of us to freeze. "Sorry, that was weird."

"No, it was... nice." It was more than just nice; it

had been so natural, and I wanted every morning to be like this with someone. Drinking coffee, laughing, tender touches, and kisses.

"I should probably get going." He went to stand up, and I grabbed his hand. He sat back down and cocked an eyebrow. "Unless you had something else in mind..."

Keeping hold of his hand, I pulled my leg onto the couch and turned toward him. "What is this?" I motioned between us. "I know you said you couldn't resist anymore, but... I need to know before I make a fool of myself."

His brows drew in, and he looked down at our clasped hands. "I... Can we not put a label on it? Let's just see where it goes."

I mulled over his words as I tapped my pencil on my sketchbook. Seeing where it went sounded like a recipe for heartbreak, but the thought of not seeing him again made my stomach turn.

I'd been down this road before and as much as I felt in my gut that I could trust Kalen with my heart which had already been glued back together once.

I lifted his chin with a finger. "Let's go to breakfast."

"Breakfast? That sounds like a date." He pulled his bottom lip between his teeth, and I used my thumb to free it. "What if someone sees us?"

"What are they going to see, Kalen? Two men out

to eat breakfast and walking around downtown? Men hang out all the time. You hang out with your buddies, don't you? I'm not asking you to hold my hand or grab my ass while we're out." I stood and pulled him to his feet. "You're supposed to show me around anyway. Let's go to your favorite breakfast spot."

Kalen's eyes searched mine. I knew last night had been a huge step for him and I was mentally preparing myself for him to brush me off. That would be the easier option for him. Hell, it would be the easier option for me too. It was so much simpler just having casual hookups, but there was something about Kalen that made me want more than that.

I was about to open my mouth and give him an out, not wanting to push too much, but then he grinned and my stomach flipped. He should really smile like that more often, it was as though his whole face lit up and ignited a twinkle in his eyes.

He winked. "I know just the place."

Living in a college town had its perks, like my townhouse being a ten-minute walk to the downtown area. Tons of restaurants, shops, and other businesses were all within walking distance of each other. The tree-lined streets and storefronts really created a small-town feel.

Kalen had been fairly quiet during our walk. I could tell he was inside his head again and it worried me. Even if he just wanted to hook up and hang out, I was fine with that, for now. But I had a feeling in the pit of my stomach that he was going to push me away again.

"Grid Masters has the best waffles in the continental United States." Kalen opened the door for me, and I walked in. The smell of sugar and waffles was overwhelming and my stomach growled. "They mix whatever you want into your waffle batter and then you can pick the toppings when it's done."

Ah, to be young again and not have to worry about what I ate. "Sounds like a true fine dining experience."

He nudged me toward the line with his elbow. "Loosen up, old man. You only live once."

"Why don't you just order for both of us?" My mouth watered as I watched an employee mix in some kind of cereal with batter for the woman in front of us. There were so many choices from simple fruit to bacon to popular kids' cereals.

Kalen ordered a waffle with pineapple, coconut, and macadamia nuts and then had them drizzle chocolate syrup on the top, plus a waffle with ham and cheese mixed inside. They came with eggs and bacon on the side.

We took our plastic number card outside to the patio that was in a courtyard with other businesses. It was already starting to heat up, and I pulled off the light jacket I'd worn. "My back's feeling better."

"Now you need to take it easy for a few more days so you don't reinjure it." He sat down across from me, his green eyes scanning the area. "You should strength train instead of just running. Running sucks balls."

Taking a sip of my water, I watched him as his eyes dropped to my throat before he looked away. "Running helps me clear my head."

"Oh, yeah? What do you need to clear your head for?" I shrugged just as the waitress came out with our food. He rubbed his hands together once she set them down. "Fuck, this looks amazing."

"Best in the continental United States?" I smirked and he unrolled his silverware from the napkin. "There's this place in San Francisco that has the best pancakes I've ever had."

We both cut into the waffle closest to us. The second the waffle mixed with ham and cheese hit my mouth, I moaned around my fork. It was unlike anything I'd ever tasted. Sweet, salty, and savory all mixed into a fluffy package.

"Good, huh?" He reached across and cut off a

piece. "Let's keep the moaning to a minimum, though."

"You don't like it when I moan?" Despite no one being within hearing distance of my low rasp, Kalen's eyes darted around like I had just divulged a state secret in a crowded room. "No one heard that, Kalen."

"I know." He cleared his throat and focused on taking a big bite of waffle.

Sighing, I did the same, staying silent despite the urge to make a sound. I couldn't help it when I tried the sweet waffle; it might actually have been the best waffle in the continental United States.

"I'm sorry," Kalen muttered, moving a piece of waffle around his plate. "I'm just being paranoid. I just keep envisioning what could happen if people found out."

"What do you think would happen?" I put my fork down and grabbed a napkin, blotting my lips. Kalen tracked my movements like a hawk. "You're looking at me right now in a way that contradicts your concerns."

His fork dropped to his plate with a clink, and he put his face in his hands. "It's like… if I suddenly grew a damn tail or something. I want to play with it, but also don't want people to laugh and call me names. Damn… that sounds really lame. Like I should be heading to the North Pole to pull Santa's sleigh or some shit."

I couldn't help it, my head dropped back and I laughed. How he went from being seen as gay, to having a tail, to being a red-nosed reindeer was pure magic. I calmed myself down and rubbed the back of my neck when I realized I was the only one laughing.

"I won't lie to you and say that there won't be people who call you names or make you feel like a pile of dog shit. It happens and it hurts so deeply that it feels like your entire world has been smashed to pieces. But what hurts even more deeply is not being who you are or being with who you want to be with." I wished I could take his hand. "I have a lot on the line here too, Kalen. I knew there wasn't anyone close enough to hear me. You don't need to worry about being outed when we're with each other."

"This is all so new to me, Monroe. I don't know how to act or feel… Jesus, what if I've really been barking up the wrong tree my entire life?" His fingers went through his hair, causing it to fall in his eyes. I moved my hands into my lap so I didn't reach across the table. "What is everyone I know going to think?"

"They'll think you're one of the bravest people they know." I cleared my throat. "I'm sorry if I've come off as a jerk… It's just…" I bit my lip and looked away.

"It's just what?" Kalen asked softly, surprising me with the sincerity in his voice. He made me feel like I could tell him anything and everything, and a lump rose in my throat.

"When I was a little younger than you are, I was in a bad relationship. The term relationship being used loosely. He was a senior… and I was a freshman. We were only together behind closed doors." It had been forever since I'd shared this with anyone. It was embarrassing and left me with a bitter taste in my mouth. "He'd always come to my dorm. Well, about seven months in, I found out he had a pregnant fiancée back home."

"Monroe, I… Wow." Kalen grabbed his water and took a long drink. "I'm sorry that happened to you."

"So, I swore to myself then that I'd never let another man hold my heart hostage like that again." I met his wide eyes and understanding flashed in them. "But then you walked into my life."

"I'm not asking for us to stay locked up in your house." He threw his napkin on his plate. "I just need to wrap my head around things before you start stealing crotch grabs when no one is looking."

"I'll let you be the first one to do a sly crotch grab. Will that work?" It had only been a week. I needed to calm down. Not everyone was an asshole out to deceive me into taking care of their sexual needs.

Once we were done, I left a tip and we headed back toward my place. It was going to be another hot day, and my skin already prickled with sweat but I couldn't tell if it was from eating so much, being near Kalen, or the sun.

As we crossed the street and walked along the edge of a park, Kalen held his arm out and stopped me abruptly. "Let's stay on the other side of the street. Those turkeys are too close to the sidewalk."

Looking at the cluster of turkeys, I laughed. "Seriously? You're scared of some turkeys?"

"A few years ago, there were warning signs posted all over town because they were attacking people for no reason. So yes, I'm scared of them unless they're stuffed and in the oven." He dropped his arm, and I moved forward, still laughing. "Monroe, I'm being serious."

"They're just turkeys! What are they even doing wandering around downtown anyway? Someone might want them for dinner." No sooner had I said the word dinner, one of the turkeys in question looked up, its beady little eyes locking on me. "See, Tom the turkey knows he's destined for the dinner table."

Flapping his wings, the turkey surged forward, heading straight for me. A godawful, ear-piercing, pants-shitting, ego-busting gobble erupted from its beak. I squealed and moved onto the grassy area of the park. But that didn't stop the damn beast from stalking toward me, its red wattle dangling like an angry old man's ballsack.

"Get away!" I shooed my hands at the bird and then he started running, wings flapping menacingly. "Fuck!"

"Run, old man!" Kalen shouted.

I took off running across the park, this giant bird that could feed a small army hot on my heels, its gobble sending a chill straight through me. Was this how I died? Had people died from a turkey attack before? Was this a hunter becoming the prey situation?

And Kalen? When I looked back over my shoulder to check the status of the bird from hell, he was laughing his ass off, wiping at his cheeks.

The playground was empty of people, thank fuck. The last thing I needed today was to have to throw a pack of toddlers in front of this wild fowl. I made a dash up the stairs of the play structure, breathing a sigh of relief when the turkey didn't follow.

I hoped me running to save my ass wasn't an indication of how Kalen and I would end up.

CHAPTER ELEVEN

Kalen

It was seven in the morning on a Saturday. *A Saturday.* And my ass was up, out of bed, and headed for the gym at the training center. My phone buzzed as I was getting off my bike, and I grinned when I saw who the message was from.

Monroe: *I'm here. You're late.*

Kalen: *Calm down, old man. It's not like you get an early bird senior discount.*

Monroe: *You're gonna pay for that sass.*

My dick twitched in my shorts, and I felt my cheeks heat. This guy was something else. He excited me in a way no one had even come close to before.

Kalen: *You gotta catch me first. *wink emoji* *running emoji**

I pushed through the doors and spotted Mr. Scowly sitting on a weight bench, his face focused on his phone screen. Since I knew he hadn't seen me, I walked around him and hit him with a sneak attack.

"Ahhh!" I grabbed his shoulder and he shrieked, his phone flying out of his hands and landing on the floor.

"Fuck, Kalen. You almost gave me a heart attack." He put his hand over his heart.

I couldn't even look at him because I was laughing so fucking hard. He charged forward and pushed me playfully which just had us laughing more. When was the last time I'd laughed like this?

"Oh my god, dude. You shrieked like a bird. Did that turkey bite you or something yesterday?" I asked and Monroe glowered, fighting a grin. "Shit, are you turning into Turkey Man? Gonna start shooting turkey wattlers out of your hands?" I busted up at the mental picture.

"Kalen, Kalen, Kalen," Monroe chided, shaking his head. "Think you're a funny guy, hmm? We'll see who's laughing later," he growled, giving me a wink that made my heart skip.

He turned and bent over to pick up his phone, his ass aimed right toward me. How easy it would be just to reach out and smack it. I stepped forward just as he stood up, his eyes meeting mine in the mirror.

"Bishop!" My name being shouted across the weight room by Baker brought me back to reality. I cringed, remembering where we were. There would be no ass grabbing this morning.

We stepped apart from each other as a couple of my friends approached, eyeing Monroe as they clapped me on the back. Shit, did they already figure out that I was *with* Monroe? Could they tell from just looking at me that I had been about to squeeze his ass?

"Fancy seeing your fine ass here." Martinez looked at the clock on the wall. "Damn, man. It's early for you, isn't it? I thought on Saturdays you needed your beauty sleep."

"This face doesn't need beauty sleep." I laughed and shoved him away when he reached to stroke my cheek. A week ago, it wouldn't have fazed me—just friends joking around—but it felt awkward with Monroe standing right there. I didn't want him to get the wrong idea.

So what if he did? We didn't have a label.

"Baker, Martinez, this is Monroe Jackson. He's a new professor here and teaches my communications class," I explained, and they fist bumped him. Watching Monroe fist bump someone wasn't something I'd ever pictured him doing, and I swallowed a snort. He was definitely more of a handshake man.

"Welcome to Alderwood. How'd you get roped

into working out with this lunatic?" Baker joked, nudging me with his shoulder.

"Ah, well... he noticed I was wincing and groaning with every movement I made, so he offered to teach me some strength training exercises for my back. I'm a runner by nature, so this is all new to me," Monroe explained easily, adding a little shrug at the end.

God, he's so cute.

Cute? What the hell?

"The beast wants to teach an injured man exercises?" Baker barked a laugh, shaking his head and addressing Monroe. "No, my man. No. Come with me, I'll show you a few things. This dude over here is a powerhouse. He could easily squat you."

"Get the fuck outta here, Bake," I chuckled.

"Yeah, Baker. You're just jealous that Kalen's squats have paid off way more than yours. Flat ass lookin' motherfucker," Martinez joked, swatting Baker's ass. Baker launched himself onto his back, wrapping him in a headlock.

"We'll be right over there, Monroe. Don't let Bishop kill you, okay? Onward, noble steed!" Baker shouted as he encouraged Martinez to move while bucking his hips against his back.

I lifted a brow and glanced over at Monroe, who was standing there with his mouth open. "What the fuck just happened?"

"You just got Baked, man. Just roll with it. Now, enough stalling. It'll be your nap time soon," I teased and Monroe lunged for me. I held my hands up in a placating fashion. "You wouldn't attack an unarmed man, would you?" I placed a hand over my heart in mock horror.

"Pretty sure you have a perfectly ample sword," he taunted, his eyes raking down my body and halting at my cock that I was certain he could see the outline of.

My face flamed with heat as I remembered the way he'd sucked on my nuts. *Shit. I can't pop a stiffy in basketball shorts.*

"Having trouble keeping your sword sheathed? I have one right here you can borrow," Monroe whispered, rubbing his thumb across his bottom lip. His eyes burned with fire. I couldn't take it.

"Be right back." The words fell out of my mouth before I could stop them, and I practically raced for the locker room. *I'm gonna jack off into the toilet like a fifteen-year-old boy. Then I'll be fit for public.*

The locker room was dead as I moved through it. I'd just passed the showers when I was pushed into one of the shower stalls from behind. The sound of the shower door clanging shut and the lock sliding into place made me remember where we were.

Spinning around, I didn't get a chance to protest before Monroe's lips smashed against mine. "You think you're a funny guy, hmm?" he grumbled, his breath warm against my mouth.

"What are you doing? We can't do this here," I whispered as his lips moved across my jaw.

"We'll be quiet." His breath tickled the sensitive skin beneath my ear and my dick jerked in my shorts. "Do you think you can handle being quiet?"

Fuck. I was so riled up that I didn't think I could tell him to stop. We were in a locked shower and the only way someone would know is if they looked under the walls or if I got loud.

Smiling like the cocky guy I was—the one who had been missing since my major league plans went up in smoke—I pushed him back and pressed him against the wall.

"I know I'm funny," I bantered back, feeling his excitement pressing against mine. Fuck, it was sexy. *He* was sexy.

"Turn around, Kalen." His eyes blazed with lust and I wanted to drown in them.

"Make me," I smirked.

Not wasting a moment, he moved fast. His hand gripped my dick and I groaned. Monroe's lips met my throat, and I almost died when he bit down.

"Fuck, Monroe," I rasped.

"Turn around, baby. And be quiet."

He stepped back from me and quickly turned the water on in the shower portion of the stall. Thank fuck for the small changing area so we didn't get wet.

"Now nobody will hear the sounds you make for me. Those are mine." Monroe stalked back to me, grabbing my shorts and boxers and pushing them down.

I stepped out of them and he put them on the changing bench. Looking at Monroe through hooded eyes, I watched, panting, as he did the same to his own clothes. His cock fell forward, heavy and hard as stone. Such a pretty dick.

What is happening to me?

"Turn around, Kalen," he ordered again. I was too fucking turned on to argue with him now, so I did as he asked. "Hands on the wall, big guy. Spread your legs."

Anticipation zapped through my fucking veins at lightspeed. *Is he going to fuck me here? Now?*

As if he heard my thoughts, he chuckled deeply. "The first time I sink into this tight virgin ass will be in a bed, on silky sheets, after I spend an hour stretching you out," he promised.

"Fuck."

"Remember to keep quiet. Otherwise, I'll have to stuff my boxers in your mouth to make sure nobody else hears."

My god. The mouth on this fucking guy. I nearly screamed out when he pushed my ass cheeks apart and buried his face in between them, his hot tongue searing a path of heat from my balls to my hole.

"Oh, Jesus. Oh, god."

"Mmm, I've wanted to do this all morning. Hold on, baby. I'm gonna rock your fucking world." He slapped my ass hard, the sound echoing in the confined space, making my cock jerk. I swallowed a whine.

Monroe's tongue worked me hard. Teasing, licking, lapping. My thighs were shaking and I wanted so badly to fist my cock, but I was afraid I'd faceplant into the wall. No, two hands were definitely required for support.

He pulled back, grabbed my hips, and turned me to face him so that my dick was right there, level with his mouth. My breaths were coming fast as I stared down in wonder at the man on his knees before me. Monroe sucked his bottom lip in between his teeth and I swear to god I almost nutted right then and there.

Lifting two fingers to his mouth, he sucked them, staring into my eyes the entire time. "Put your leg on my shoulder, baby."

I did. Oh my god, I did it so fast.

His mouth was on my aching cock in an instant. His groan of appreciation vibrated around me and I felt my balls tighten. Monroe must've realized how close I was because he wrapped his thumb and index finger around the base of my balls and pulled them down away from my body.

"Fuuuuck. Monroe. Jesus."

"Not yet," he grunted, his hand furiously pumping his own dick. So. Fucking. Hot.

My head dropped back against the tiles, and I nearly floated off the ground when his fingers started teasing my ass. Swirling, seeking.

This man very well might kill me. Sign me the fuck up.

CHAPTER TWELVE

Monroe

My dick was running the show, and I wasn't about to complain. When Kalen had rushed off to the locker room, I knew exactly what he was planning on doing with the impressive bulge in his shorts.

Should I have accosted him in the locker room? Probably not. Was I going to make him come and risk us being caught? Absolutely.

He was so fucking sexy, spread open in front of me, his dick so hard it was weeping tears of joy. I gathered his precum on my finger and continued teasing his tight hole, looking up at him as he nearly came undone.

His hands sought to find anything they could

grab onto, one taking hold of my hair, the other first clawing at the glossy white tiles, and then raising to his mouth in a fist.

Lapping at his tip, I pushed just the tip of my finger in, gauging his reaction. We hadn't talked about whether he'd engaged in anal play before, but I'd fathom a guess he hadn't.

"Monroe." His voice was muffled by his fist he was biting into but his cock jerked against my lips.

I sucked the head of his cock into my mouth, moving my free hand to his taint, where I pressed my thumb. His fingers tightened in my hair, the pain of it making my cock harder than stone.

"Are you good?" My finger continued to tease him.

"Just fucking do it and get that sexy mouth back on my cock," he gritted out, his eyes smoldering as they looked down at me.

Fuck. I wished we were at my place.

"Relax." I kissed up his shaft from root to tip before taking him all the way to the back of my throat, pressing my finger past the tight ring of muscle.

A strangled gasp left him as I began fingering him, hitting his prostate with each thrust. His legs trembled and his shoulders sagged against the wall.

The shower door next to us closed and locked and Kalen tensed, his ass squeezing around my finger. I continued taking him to the back of my throat, running my tongue along the underside as I pulled away, and swallowing as I pushed forward.

The water turned on and someone started humming, no clue that two men were about to come undone in the stall next to him.

Kalen's ass pushed against my finger and he stifled his moans with his hand over his mouth. His dick hit the back of my throat at the same time I pressed on his taint and prostate, and I damn near felt like he was going to yank out my hair.

His hot cum spilled down my throat, rope after rope of his pleasure becoming my prize. I pumped my cock, watching him as he came down from his peak.

"I'll—" he started on a whisper but then I was coming, my own release nearly causing me to fall sideways into the spray of the shower.

Chest heaving, I stood and put my forehead against his. "Next time I make you come like that, I'll be buried inside you."

"I—" Kalen started, but I brushed my lips against his, silencing him. We kissed for a few minutes, and then I backed away, going to the shower and washing my hands.

He pulled on his boxers and shorts, and handed me my own to put on. Whoever had been humming in the stall next to us had finished their shower, but I had no idea if he had left yet.

"I'll go out first and you can follow." I poked my head out of the door and looked down the row of showers and changing stalls. Since it was a Saturday, luckily there weren't many people at the gym in the first place.

Quickly walking out of the shower area and through the rest of the room which held lockers, I was almost home free when I ran smack dab into Baker. "Oh shit, Monroe, slow down. You all right?"

Was I all right? Hell no. Had I taken even a few seconds longer, he probably would have seen me coming out of the shower area looking like I hadn't taken a shower... and then seen Kalen.

I barked out a laugh, gave him a pat on the chest, and moved around him quickly, spotting Kalen just coming out of the shower area as I turned the corner out of the locker room.

Hopefully, Baker wouldn't put two and two together. Would it even matter? Kalen seemed to be really close with his friends and it didn't seem like it would matter to them if he was messing around with me.

But of course, I had come to realize that just because someone appears like they would understand doesn't mean they do. It's a completely different thing when they actually know someone who's gay. There had been a few times where I'd come out to friends or colleagues that hadn't known, and been blindsided by their reactions.

Making my way back to the weights, I tried to re-energize myself for working out. After the orgasm I'd had, all I really wanted to do was lie down and stare at the ceiling. My limbs were still tingly and I could still feel the beating of my heart in my ears.

Kalen finally made his way out of the locker room and sauntered over to me, looking sexy as fuck. He gave me a light smile and grabbed a few dumbbells off the rack. "Ready to get started?"

"I ran into your buddy on my way out. Everything okay there?"

Kalen shrugged. "He gave me a funny look, but he didn't ask me any questions. I went to my locker and acted like I was getting something. We should probably be more careful." Now that I was closer to him, I could see that he had a slightly panicked expression on his face.

"Well, he seems like a pretty forward man. I think if he thought anything, he would've said something outright. Right?" I knew that this wasn't necessarily true, but maybe it would give some comfort to Kalen and whatever was going on inside of his brain.

"Yeah… Let's get busy. I can't have you not being able to keep up with me, old man."

My entire body felt like it had been assaulted and we had barely used any weight for the strength training exercises he'd shown me. Most of the time was spent on proper form with no weight. I knew his exercises were going to help me become a better runner, but I wasn't looking forward to feeling the effects of them in the morning.

We headed out of the training center and stopped at the bike rack, where Kalen pulled his keys out of his backpack and unlocked his bike. "What are you doing tonight?"

I was honestly a little surprised he'd asked. We'd already spent the last few days together, and I'd expected him to want to spend time with his friends. I was just opening my mouth to tell him that I had a prior engagement when his phone went off.

"Shit, I have to get this. It's my dad." Kalen blew out a shaky breath and pulled his phone out of his bag, swiping to accept the call. "Hello?"

He walked away from me, just out of earshot, but I could tell by the way his shoulders suddenly hunched that the conversation he was having with his dad wasn't a good one. After what he'd told me at breakfast the day before, he wanted to make his dad proud but no matter what he did, it was never good enough.

It was a fairly short call, less than two minutes, but when he turned around, he looked like he'd been talking to his father for several hours. What the hell had the man said?

Shaking his head, he shoved his phone in his backpack and ran a hand down his face. "Is it too early to start drinking?"

"That bad?" I wished I could take all of his problems, bag them up, and throw them into the deepest part of the ocean.

That realization—and so quickly after just meeting him—put me on edge. I was already on a slippery slope of questionable judgment when it came to him. So many things could have gone wrong with what we just did in the locker room, yet I'd done it anyway.

"I don't want to talk about it. So… tonight?" He yanked his bike out of the bike rack and threw his leg over it. "Maybe we grab a drink then head to your place."

"I actually have a work thing this evening that I have to go to. I'm not sure how late it will be, but want me to call you when I'm done?" I pulled my car keys out of my pocket and flipped them back and forth in my hand. "We probably should skip the drinking part."

Kalen shrugged. "If you want to. I should get going. This hard ass professor gave us two chapters to read over the weekend, and I have an essay due soon."

I laughed. "Professors have no soul. Who would choose such a career unless they wanted to watch impressionable minds fold under pressure?"

I looked around, but there were too many people to give Kalen anything other than just a friendly wave goodbye. I didn't know how long I could last keeping us a secret. Even if we were just having fun and seeing where things went, I didn't want to hide.

Mingling with work colleagues wasn't exactly what I'd call an exciting Saturday evening, but somehow it turned out to be a good time. Once a month, my department had a mixer that included dinner and drinks for anyone that wanted to attend. It was a good way to meet new people and form collaborative relationships for research and instruction.

"Grady and I are going to head to Slugger's for a drink or two. Care to join us?" Simon, a professor who was a few years older than me asked, as the mixer came to an end. He was a good-looking man, with an aura and personality that was the life of the party.

"Sure." It was only nine. I could have a few drinks,

then call Kalen to see if he still wanted to hang out. "It's right down the street, isn't it?"

"Yup! All of downtown is walkable." We headed out the door where Grady was waiting. "Didn't you say you live close?"

"Just past downtown. It was a nice ten-minute walk here."

We headed down the street and were just about at our destination when Grady's phone rang. He cursed and sighed as he answered. "Yes, hon? No, just one... but... well, fuck." He pulled the phone away from his ear and looked at the screen. "Be home in ten."

We stopped walking and Simon put his hands on his hips. "She wants the D, doesn't she?"

Grady held his arms out as if to say "what can I say?" and laughed. "Since the baby, she hasn't wanted it much, so I take it any chance I can get. Raincheck?"

We waved goodbye and walked the last block to the bar. As Grady hustled down the sidewalk in the opposite direction, I felt Simon's stare.

"Guess it's just us then, hmm?" he mused. I felt the heat in his gaze, and maybe—no, definitely—under normal circumstances, I'd be interested in messing around. That was the pre-Kalen Monroe, though. Things had changed abruptly and that freaked me out. Exclusivity wasn't something that I'd even entertained the thought of in a very long time.

"Looks that way. Come on, I'm jonesing for a whiskey."

We strode side by side up to the bar and I held the door open for Simon. Just because I didn't want to sleep with the man didn't mean I shouldn't be a gentleman. *I'll just have a couple of drinks and then I'll text Kalen to see what he's up to.* My feelings for him were growing stronger, and my brain was at war. *You're fucking around with a closeted man. This won't end well.*

My body didn't want to listen to reason. No, Kalen Bishop had gotten under my skin. He was unexpected, the intensity with which I wanted him insane. But when I walked into the bar behind Simon, the last thing I expected to see was Kalen with his little *girl* friend perched in his lap.

CHAPTER THIRTEEN

Kalen

After the gym, I returned home and took a quick shower. I did have some reading to do, and I needed to get started on my assignment. Schoolwork was not something I liked. Ever. But I found myself eager to complete the work. Probably because in a way, it made me feel connected to Monroe.

This was something he enjoyed. Enough to become a professor in the subject. Not to mention, ever since he'd started giving me pointers and tips for studying, and taking the extra time to discuss the material with me in a way that I understood, I'd gotten a boost in confidence. For the first time, it felt like things were clicking in my brain, and I was retaining the information.

It was a little after two when there was a knock at my bedroom door. I was sprawled out on my bed, and looked up from my laptop, telling whoever it was to come in. Baker slipped into the room and flopped down beside me on the bed.

"Whatcha doing?" he asked, clearly knowing I was working on homework.

"Stuff for Monroe's class. What's up?" I glanced over and found him studying me intently. "What?" I asked when he just kept staring. Did I have something on my face?

"Monroe seems cool," he commented.

"Yeah. I didn't care for him at first, but he's a nice guy." I started gathering up my things to call it a day.

"What's going on with you two?"

What? My eyes darted to his, and I quickly looked down, busying myself with my task so I wouldn't have to look at him.

"What do you mean? He's my friend," I said, going for calm and collected. Pretty sure I failed, though.

"Bishop. I walked into the locker room, and I know the vibes that were going on in there," he said softly, like he was speaking to a spooked horse. His brown eyes were sincere, but this wasn't something I wanted to discuss with anyone. Let alone the giant, blond third baseman.

"I don't know what you think you saw or picked up on, but I feel like you're insinuating that I was fucking around with my professor. My *male* professor." I lowered my voice, suddenly feeling defensive. "I'm not gay, Baker."

He held up his hands in surrender. "Didn't say that you were, man. There is such a thing as bisexuality. I'd know since I'm bi," he confessed and my mouth dropped open.

"What?"

"I'm bi. Have been for as long as I can remember. It's not something I broadcast because really, who I fuck is my business. I just wanted to say that if things were happening and you needed someone to talk to, you know I got your back." He clapped me on the shoulder and smiled.

He was bi? What the hell? I still couldn't tell him about Monroe. Also, if he'd picked up on it that easily, I was concerned that others might, too. It wasn't just about not wanting anyone to know that I was sleeping with a man—Monroe was my professor and could get in serious trouble if it was discovered. No. I needed a cover.

"Good for you, dude. Thanks for telling me," I said, looking around the room. My panic caused the next words to flow from my big mouth. "I'm with Nikki."

Baker's eyebrows lifted to his hairline before his eyes narrowed. "Nikki is a lesbian, Kalen."

"Wrong. She's bi. And we're dating. Now, if you'll excuse me, I have to call her and see what time she's meeting me at Slugger's later. Feel free to join us," I offered, walking over to the door to let him out. Sweat was trailing down my spine and I felt nauseous.

"Good talk, Bishop. See ya later then," he grumbled, as he walked past me and out of my room.

I was such a dick. My friend just came out to me in an attempt to make me comfortable, and I'd acted like a total shithead. Fuck.

My phone started going off, the dreaded ringtone that I hated hearing.

"Dad," I said as I picked up the phone.

"How was practice this morning?"

Great. Nice to hear from you too, Dad. I rolled my eyes.

"No practice this morning. I worked out," I told him as I kept pacing around my room.

He scoffed. "You need to be practicing every day. You know that. You're never going to get anywhere worthwhile being lazy."

My jaw was flexing so hard I worried I was going to chip a tooth. He'd already called earlier to meddle in my life. Telling me all about scouts he'd reached out to in light of my recent failure. There was still hope, he'd said.

"I'm going to the cages later. I had some school stuff to take care of this morning, too," I reminded him. *I'm still a fucking college student. Schoolwork comes with the territory.*

"Right. Summer school. Another waste of—" His voice cut off, and I heard him speaking to someone. It was hard to make out what he was saying, but he sounded angry. Not that that was anything new for him. He lived in a constant state of bitterness.

"Your nephew is here. Showed up wearing nail polish and eyeliner. Eyeliner, Kalen. Who have I wronged so grievously to have a grandson who wears makeup? Thank god he's only thirteen. Plenty of time to turn that trainwreck around. Now, where were we?"

I wasn't even listening anymore. All I could hear was whooshing in my ears. My dad did not support equal rights and was one of the biggest homophobes I'd ever met. Of course, he hid this from the public, saving his true thoughts for his family, behind closed doors.

After another minute of me replying to whatever he was saying with just "mmhmm" and other sounds of acknowledgment, he must have said bye because suddenly my phone beeped with a new text message.

Fuck. My dad would probably beat my ass if he

found out I'd been seeing a man. It was bad enough that my nephew had to be exposed to his shit. My dad couldn't find out. Ever.

With renewed purpose, I opened my messages and saw one from Nikki, asking about going out. Perfect. Replying quickly, I told her to come over immediately. I could trust her. She was my best friend and I needed her help. Desperately.

"I SWEAR TO GOD, Kalen. This better be good. I left the curviest mamacita you've ever seen in my bed to come over here," Nikki complained as she walked into my room. I quickly darted over and shut the door behind her. "Okaaaay. You're being extra weird today. What the hell is going on?" she questioned, eyeing me like I might flip out at any moment. Which was true. I might.

"I need you to do something for me," I said, shakily.

Her eyes widened and she nodded. "What is it? Are you in trouble? Who do I need to stab? I can run back to my house and grab my ax."

I choked on a laugh that was basically half a sob. My ferocious best friend actually competed in ax throwing competitions when she wasn't busy playing ball or chasing chicks.

"I need you to be my girlfriend," I blurted out, and we both stood there frozen for a moment before she threw her head back and cackled.

"Are you on drugs?" she asked, dead serious.

"No," I scoffed. "I'm not on drugs. I'm being serious."

Nikki studied my face for a few moments, clearly trying to see if I was bullshitting her or not. Eventually, she saw the truth and sighed. "What the fuck is going on, Kalen?" She walked over and grabbed me by the arm, dragging me over to the bed and pulling me down to sit beside her.

"I…" *Come on, just fucking tell her.*

"You know you can tell me anything. It's okay," she said softly.

"Last Friday night when I was at the bar with the guys? I picked someone up. Fucked around in a hotel room," I admitted, looking down at the bedspread.

"Okay, and this is a new development for you? You fuck around all the time." She laughed, but it held a note of nervousness.

"It was with a guy," I confessed.

"It was a g—" She stopped herself mid-sentence as her mouth fell open. "It was a guy!" she screeched, launching herself at me and hugging me tightly. I noted that there wasn't a question there—she didn't sound surprised.

"Yes. And as it turns out, he's my professor," I said, grimacing.

"Monroe Jackson? You're fucking around with Monroe Jackson? Baby, I'm as straight as a serrated knife and even I can admire that man's gorgeousness. Holy shit!" Nikki was jumping up and down on my bed now, doing toe touches and grinning down at me.

"You don't seem… surprised?"

"I'm not. Not really, I mean. A little surprised that you actually did it," she said, dropping down to the bed on her ass.

My brow furrowed. "What does that mean? That I act gay?"

"No, that would be kinda stereotypical of me to say. Gay just calls to gay, okay?" She shrugged, like this wasn't a huge fucking deal. "It's hard for me to explain. I've just always gotten the sense that you aren't that into women. Anytime we're talking about women when we're out, you seem… bored. You can fuck them but that doesn't mean shit at the end of the day."

"Whatever. Look. This is why I need you to be my girlfriend. I'm still seeing Monroe but I don't want anyone to get suspicious. If I have a girlfriend, then people won't know," I said quickly, hoping she would understand.

She threw her head back and laughed. "I'm sorry.

Really. You want me to be your beard? Kalen, I'm a lesbian! This is common knowledge. Half of Sorority Row will confirm that fact."

"You can say we're best friends, and you suddenly realized you had feelings for me. Look, it doesn't have to be for long, and only in public every so often. For example, tonight. At Slugger's." I wiped a hand down my face, overwhelmed with everything at this point.

"Fine. But I'm not your girlfriend—we're just casually dating. No kissing. Those are my terms. And no cunt-blocking or so help me…" she threatened, shaking her fist in my direction but I was already grinning.

This was going to work. What a fucking relief.

"So, who bottoms?"

…goddammit.

"So, it just happened all of a sudden? Out of nowhere?" Martinez took a large ass gulp of his beer and narrowed his eyes at me and Nikki. He'd gone through a full range of emotions since I'd pulled her onto my lap.

Yeah. We were trying to fucking sell it, but my asshole friends were giving me a hard time.

Everyone except Baker. Baker was quieter than a house mouse on a mission.

"Yup." Nikki pinched my cheek. "I just can't get enough of the big guy, if you know what I'm saying. We're keeping it casual."

I laughed and squeezed her waist for the hundredth time. "Yeah, we're both super busy and don't want to end up falling in love or anything like that. Although..." I looked up at her.

She hit my chest playfully. "Oh, stop it."

Nikki didn't have a career in Hollywood ahead of her. Her idea of pretending to be seeing each other was taking on a Barbie-like tone of voice.

"I don't buy it." Baker threw back the rest of his beer and shook his head. "I'm going to head out."

"After just one?" Martinez frowned. "Is everyone out of it tonight or what? Is it a full moon?"

I didn't know what had crawled up Baker's ass, but the last thing I needed was for him to out me to everyone. I hadn't told him, but I felt like he knew and was holding it in. He wouldn't let it slip, would he?

"On second thought, I think I'm going to stay." Baker had been starting to stand but flopped back down, reaching for the pitcher of beer. "Hey, isn't that your communications professor?"

I stiffened and my heart damn near jumped out

of my chest. Monroe? Monroe was here at Slugger's? What the hell?

"Oh man, this is perfect. I like that dude. Monroe, over here!" Martinez waved his arm in the air.

"Dude, no," I said between gritted teeth, grabbing for his arm.

"Yeah, Martinez, don't. Looks like he's on a date or something." Baker's eyes were locked on me as he sipped his beer. What the fuck? Was Monroe trying to make me jealous? Because it was fucking working.

Do not turn around, Kalen. Do. Not. Turn—

I heard Monroe's husky laugh and couldn't resist. I did it. I looked, and I squeezed Nikki so tight she had to cover her gasp with a cough.

Didn't he say he had a work function and would text me after? Was that work function sliding his cock into some guy's ass?

The man he was with was attractive—definitely not my type though—and had a hand on his arm.

Not my type? I had a type?

I grabbed my beer and pounded it as my friends continued on with their conversation about a new movie or some shit. Me? All I really wanted to do was go rip that guy's hand from my man's arm and bend Monroe over the stool and—

"Hey... are you all right?" Nikki put her hand on my cheek, and I was brought back to reality. She kept her voice low as she leaned into me. "Maybe they aren't on a date."

Why did I even care if it *was?* I told him we shouldn't put a label on us, yet here I was going apeshit inside over him having a drink with a guy. A very attractive guy who was way too close to him.

"I'm fine."

Perfectly fine.

CHAPTER FOURTEEN

Monroe

What the fuck is he doing with her on his lap?
My good mood was quickly dashed away as I spotted Kalen in a booth on the opposite side of the bar with the girl from the other day... on his lap. She threw her head back in a laugh and Kalen looked up at her with a cocky grin lighting his face.

My stomach bottomed out at the sight, and I had a brief flash of me walking over there and asking him what the fuck he was doing in front of the girl and the rest of his buddies. He would splutter through his words, turning red in the face, and his friends would stare slack-jawed at the drama unfolding before their very eyes.

But I didn't, because I was an adult. An adult who should have never let myself get involved with someone so young in the first place.

I tried not to stare for too long at how his hand was wrapped around her and how happy they looked together. Had he been gaslighting me this whole time?

Anger swirled in my stomach as I marched past Simon to take a seat at the bar where I could see them clearly. I thought I heard my name called, but when I turned to see, Simon gave me a funny look.

He slid onto the stool next to me. "You look like you just found out Lady Gaga doesn't think we were born this way." He put his hand on my arm and gave it a squeeze.

"She would never." I threw my head back and laughed. When really, on the inside I was screaming. Why did it matter if he was out with some chick? We were nothing.

Yeah, right.

"What's eating you, Monroe?" My attention was brought back to Simon, who had a smirk on his face that was hinting at something else.

"Nothing. Just really need a drink."

I could tell him what wasn't eating me. That six-foot-one baseball god with his hands all over a woman. Not even twelve hours ago, I'd had his dick in my mouth and those same hands of his buried in my fucking hair.

"What can I get for you, handsome?" The bartender's flirting was on point, but she was barking up the wrong tree.

"Whiskey neat, please. Make it a double." My eyes were still on Kalen across the room. The view of him was almost perfect, besides the chick blocking his face with her body.

"I'll take your house IPA." Simon cleared his throat. "So... tell me about yourself."

"Not much to tell. I just moved here. I was an adjunct faculty member for a year after finishing my Ph.D. and decided to find a tenure track position. I've just been getting settled and learning the lay of the land."

With my attention half on Simon, I looked back over at Kalen. His fist was wrapped tightly around a beer glass and he was leaned back just enough to see around his girl. She put her hand on his cheek and leaned close.

"I see someone has caught your eye." Simon sighed. "Didn't take you for the type to like athletes. They're bad news though. You're better off going into the city to the clubs. There are about four places within walking distance from each other that are decent enough."

I barely processed a word he was saying. "Finding

someone at the club is better?" I looked over at him to find him also staring intently at the table in question. "Looks like someone has caught your eye too."

His eyes snapped to mine, and he let out a hearty laugh. "Been there, done that. It's fun for the night, but dating an athlete? How depressing."

"Why do you say that?" This conversation was a nice distraction from Kalen but didn't sound like it was in my favor.

"They're so busy, and who knows how far they'll go into professional play. Doesn't really bode well for serious relationships. Do you see the one with the unfortunate man bun?" I nodded, and he sighed. "I met him through one of the apps last year. Hung out a few times, fooled around a little, then he said he didn't want to start anything because of baseball, but then I see him all the time with girls hanging all over him. Seems like he doesn't even remember me."

Baker? I would have never known he was bisexual. He clearly liked attention from the ladies and sextivities with them. I wondered if Kalen knew he was bi.

"Well, you did meet him on an app—that was your first mistake." I looked back over at the table to see Kalen shrugging his shoulders. He grabbed his beer glass which was three-fourths full, drank it in one go, and slammed the glass on the table.

Unease washed over me as he scooted out of the

booth, setting his girl on her feet, and heading straight for me and Simon.

Fuck. *What are you doing, Kalen?*

He came to stand at the bar right on the other side of me, just as Simon said, "I'm ready for a relationship, aren't you?"

Kalen made a strangled noise in his throat, then turned and practically ran out of the bar.

Shit. Why the fuck is he storming out of here like someone just railed him with no lube?

"Ugh, sorry man. I need to go. Maybe I'll see you around campus?" I quickly pulled a twenty from my wallet.

Trying not to make it obvious that I was rushing after Kalen, I tried to keep my stride reasonable until I got outside. I looked both ways and spotted him already a block away, his hands in his hair and his shoulders hunched.

He rounded the corner, and I upped my pace. He didn't get to storm out of the bar and leave without acknowledging that he'd led me on. And for what? For a better grade? To test the waters?

"Kalen!" He didn't stop or turn around. I wasn't sure I was going to catch him if he took off running. I might have been a runner but he trained for sprints. "Bishop!"

"Fuck! What?" He turned around, and his features were pinched tight. "Just go the fuck back to the bar.

That guy looked like your type. Some work function that must have been."

"What..." I took a calming breath. "You have the gall to stand here and be mad at me? I walk in and you have some chick on your lap, whispering sweet nothings in your ear! Just this morning I had my finger in your—"

"Shut up, Monroe. Just shut up!" His face was red, and he looked about ready to lose his shit. Or had he already lost it? "Nikki? She's a friend." He ran his hand down his face. "Jesus, who did you think she was?"

"Someone that sits on their man's lap." I crossed my arms. "I told you I wasn't going to play these games, Kalen. Yet here we are."

"I'm not playing a game!" Before I could even register what he was doing, he pushed me against the window of a storefront, his arms on either side of my head. "Nikki is into chicks. We're pretending to date because Baker was already asking questions."

That didn't make me feel any better, and I cringed. "And I'm just supposed to know that? I don't care if she's into unicorns, I wasn't going to sit and watch her wiggle around on your lap all night. Pretending or not."

"So you decide to get back at me by hooking up with some guy?" He backed up, his eyes glossy with hurt. Since when was having a drink signs of a hookup? Was it because that was the way we'd met in the first place? "You talk about me playing games, yet you're the master."

"I'm not playing a game, Kalen. I'm allowed to have a drink with a work colleague. He wasn't sitting on my lap, was he?" Shaking my head, I headed toward my house.

"Monroe." He jogged after me and we fell into step. "I didn't like seeing you talk to another guy, all right? Let's just... start over."

I stopped and he stepped closer to me, our faces inches from each other. The man was giving me whiplash with his feelings. Maybe our connection was too good to be true and this... whatever it was, was dead in the water.

"What are you doing?" I whispered as he brought his hand to my face. There wasn't anyone on the sidewalk we were on, but that didn't mean someone wouldn't come around the corner any second.

His thumb ran across my bottom lip, pulling it away from my teeth before trailing it down to where my shirt was unbuttoned at the top. My eyes shut as he leaned closer, and his lips brushed across my ear.

My entire body thrummed with awareness of the way his hand gently brushed against my hip and his thudding pulse in his other hand that was now against my cheek. Why was he torturing me like this?

"I like you more than just friends. Okay, Monroe?" He kept his lips against the shell of my ear, and I shivered as they brushed against it. "I don't know what to do with what I'm feeling."

"Stop worrying about what everyone is going to think if they find out. We can be discreet, but at the end of the day, if people find out, then they fucking find out." I took a step back, and his fingers lingered on my cheek. "You don't want people who aren't supportive of you in your life."

"You're right, I don't." He sighed and then a slow smile spread across his face. "Let's go back to your place."

"As much as I want to do that, right now, I think we need to take a step back. What happened tonight is going to keep happening. I know we said we'd see where things go, but Kalen? I can't. I can't go through this with another man."

"That's what I was trying to tell you... I don't want to just fool around. I want to date." He let out a shaky breath and ran a hand through his hair, giving it a just rolled out of bed appearance. "Let's go on a date. A real one."

I studied his face as we stood there in the middle of the sidewalk, the light from a streetlamp illuminating his face, making him look ethereal. It was scaring me how easily he could get under my skin, how quickly I felt comfortable with him.

How quickly I felt... at home.

I'd been used once before and I'd sworn it would never happen again. "And then what, Kalen? You freak out and kiss your friend to cover up who you are? You take my heart and rip it to shreds? I need you to be sure."

"I'm sure." He pulled his bottom lip between his teeth. "Let me show you how sure. When are you free for me to take you out?"

"You're going to take *me* out?" Why did my face feel like it was burning? "What about Thursday?"

"Perfect. I'll pick you up at eight." His eyes darted up and down the street, and then he stepped forward, brushing his lips against my cheek and then my ear. "I can't wait."

He headed back in the direction of the bar, and I stood there wondering what the fuck had just happened.

CHAPTER FIFTEEN

Kalen

I'd spent the week focused on baseball. The freshmen had arrived and our practices were lengthy and intense. Each morning, I'd go to class and try to focus on Monroe's lecture, but damn, it was difficult. The more I saw him, the more I wanted him. We'd texted some, but between baseball and homework, I was pretty much dead to the world by seven o'clock and passed out by eight.

As the week crept closer to Thursday, the nerves amped up. Every time I thought about our upcoming date, my stomach flip-flopped like a salmon out of water. I'd been on my fair share of dates—the standard dinner and a movie, or grabbing a drink at a bar—but this was an entirely different ball game.

Monroe had shown uncertainty on Saturday night after the Nikki incident. I felt like this was my chance to prove that I was interested and dedicated to seeing what was growing between us. I'd driven myself crazy trying to put together the perfect date and I still wasn't sure I'd gotten it right. Time would tell, I guess.

There was also the fact that Monroe was eight years older than me. He'd been hurt before, and the thought of him with another guy had my hands clenching and my jaw ticking. Maybe he'd call the entire thing off since I was so much younger. Fuck, I hoped not.

Practice today had been exhausting. Once I got home, I flopped on my bed for a solid two hour nap and woke up feeling much better. Freshly showered, I dug through my clothes, tossing nearly everything I owned onto the bed.

Finally, I found a pair of jeans and slipped them on. Staring at myself in the mirror, I turned in a circle. My fashion choices were almost solely athletic wear. It was easier and more comfortable. I hadn't worn a pair of jeans in forever and the ones I pulled out of my closet were a little snug against my legs and ass. At least I knew my workouts were paying off.

I bit my lip and let out a frustrated groan. The shirt was all wrong.

Ripping it over my head, I considered if I should just text Monroe and cancel… or tell him I was just going to head to his place to give him a blow job. Why go on a date when we could just skip to the good part?

There was a knock on my bedroom door as I stomped out of my bathroom and slid open my closet door. "Come in." I threw the offending shirt on the floor and began rummaging through my shirt options.

"Hey, man." Baker poked his head in. "Jeans? I didn't think you owned any. Got a hot date?"

"Either get out, or shut up and help me find something to wear." I grabbed a hanger with a polo shirt probably from when I was in high school and held it up against my chest. "I feel like a chick right now."

Baker stuffed his hands in his pockets as he crossed the room. "Going out with Monroe?"

"No, with Nikki." I backed up a step as he moved in front of my closet. "I don't want to fuck this up."

"I don't think *Nikki* will care what you're wearing." He grabbed a button up. "Keep the top three buttons undone and roll the sleeves up. It's a hot look."

Snorting a response, I snatched it from him and then sighed. "Look… I'm going through some shit right now, and I'm sorry if—"

"Cut the shit, man. It doesn't matter if you are going through shit. I thought we were best friends, but you can't even be honest with me when I ask you who you're going out with."

"Why does it matter?" I slipped my arms in the shirt and started buttoning it.

Baker smacked my hands out of the way and undid the misaligned buttons. "Because you're fucking shaking, you're so nervous about your date. Maybe if you had someone to talk to truthfully about it, you wouldn't be so nervous."

He was right—I was being an asshole. I didn't know why I couldn't just tell him. It wasn't like he was going to blab it to the world that I was going on a date with a man. I could trust Baker. Hell, he was in the same situation as I was. Except for the whole professor thing.

"What if he doesn't like me?" I watched as he buttoned me up. "He's eight years older than me. What are we going to even talk about?"

Baker finished his task and sat down on my bed. "There's plenty to talk about. Baseball, when he was in college, movies, music, vacations. You've already hung out with him, haven't you?"

Rolling up my sleeves, I moved back into the bathroom to make sure I didn't look ridiculous. "A little, but what if we run out of things to talk about?"

"Where is he taking you?" Baker lay back on my

bed, a baseball flying into the air as he threw it up and caught it.

"I'm taking him to dinner and then to one of those paint night things. He likes to paint flowers so I figured he'd like painting a landscape too. Is it a dumb idea?" The best part about it was it was in the city about thirty miles from campus, so I could relax a little more. Not that I planned on sticking my tongue down his throat in public or anything.

"Sounds like a great idea, man. I bet he'll love it," Baker replied and I released a sigh. Strangely, I did feel better now that I'd come clean to him about Monroe. His support and reassurance was doing wonders for my anxiety.

"All right, I'm heading out," I announced, patting my ass to make sure I had my wallet.

"Have fun. Be safe," Baker said with a wink that had my cheeks flaming with heat.

Flipping him the bird, I waited for him to walk out of my room before I followed, shutting the door behind me.

Here goes nothing.

I KNOCKED AND WAITED, my stomach doing the fucking Macarena with anticipation. What if he'd changed his mind? What if this was all too much risk for Monroe? Before I could deep dive further into self-doubt, the door swung open.

"Kalen," he purred in that deep, seductive voice. Fuck. "You're early."

"Hi," I chirped lamely. That was the only thing I could think to say because I was focused on the man before me.

God, he was gorgeous. His dark wash jeans were skintight and a light blue button up shirt fit his slim frame perfectly. Dark hair was styled so it looked somehow like it wasn't. His blue eyes seemed to be appreciating the view of me, too.

"You look nice," I said, stepping inside and giving him a quick peck on the mouth.

Monroe looked at me as though I was a puzzle he needed to put together. "Thank you. You look sinful in those jeans. Your ass. Jesus, Kalen," he rasped out when I walked away from him, further into the townhouse.

"Squats. Lots and lots of squats. Life of a catcher," I replied with a grin.

"Well, hallelujah for squats," he chuckled, flashing his perfectly white teeth.

I was always so nervous leading up to being near Monroe and yet, the moment I was in his company, all of that disappeared.

"So, what's the plan?" Monroe asked, leaning against the island in his kitchen.

"Hmm, I think I'll keep that a surprise. For now," I teased, matching his stance on the opposite side of the counter.

One dark brow lifted. "That's how you want to play it?"

I hummed in pretend thought. "Yeah. Yeah, I think that's how I'll play it. What are you going to do about it?"

"Tie you to the bed and make you talk?" Monroe blurted out and my mouth popped open. Oh shit, he was serious. My dick liked that idea entirely too much.

"Nuh-uh. We have reservations. Time to go!" I moved for the door and he pounced. Quite literally.

His lean body pressed against my back, his hard cock pressing right against the crack of my ass.

"It's going to be hard to keep my hands off of you when you're looking so delicious," he whispered in my ear and I released a barely audible groan.

"I'm going to show you I'm good boyfriend material. Now, you're going to have to save the cock grabbing for after our date, old man," I teased and he released me with a scoff.

"I'll show you old man," he muttered, a wicked gleam in his eye.

Please do.

We arrived at the restaurant right on time, which was a miracle considering how handsy my date was being. The entire drive, Monroe had been teasing me with little touches, caressing my arm while I drove, holding my hand.

I would've thought he had no idea the effect he was having on me, but then I'd see the smug ass smirk on his face and I knew what he was doing. Seduction. Winding me up higher and higher. If he kept it up, by the time we got to his house later, I'd be ready to explode.

"I hope this place is okay." I locked my car and walked beside Monroe to the door of the restaurant. I sped up to get slightly in front so I could open it for him. "After you, my lady."

"Hm. We'll see if you're calling me a lady later tonight." His voice promised that I'd be paying for that, and I wasn't opposed. My cock was already twitching in my pants.

After giving the hostess my name, we were led to a table with a view of the street. If things got awkward or we ran out of things to talk about, at least we could people watch.

"You didn't have to bring me to such a fancy place." Monroe opened his menu and made a satisfied sound in the back of his throat. "Good choice, though."

"This is my first grown up date." He looked at me

over the top of his menu, and I blushed. "You know what I mean."

"I don't, actually. All dates are grown up." He kept his eyes on me, and I shifted in my seat. "You don't have to impress me by taking me to expensive places."

"But I want to." Clearing my throat, I looked at my own menu. I already knew what I wanted; I'd stalked the online menu earlier to make sure I didn't make a rash decision that was too far off my nutrition plan. "I think I'll be skipping the Rocky Mountain oysters."

"They sound right up my alley." He smirked and then laughed as I twisted my mouth in disgust. I enjoyed trying new things but bull's balls were where I drew the line. I didn't care if they were deep fried.

The waiter came back with our drinks and took our order, leaving us with the most delicious smelling bread to gorge on. Damn it.

"This smells amazing. Do you think it's the best bread this side of the Mississippi?" His grin made butterflies erupt in my stomach. He'd already picked up on my little quirk and was taking pleasure in teasing me about it.

"There's a lot of bread in the world, but this is probably the best within a hundred mile radius." I ripped a piece in half and put it on my appetizer plate.

"You're only going to eat half a piece?" He raised an eyebrow.

"I need to tighten up my diet since training's in full swing. The freshmen who just started training with us are amazing. They absorb shit like sponges." Instead of taking a bite of his bread, his attention was solely on me as I talked. "Like this kid, Sanchez. He has an arm on him but I've been working with him on getting a better break on his curveball. I gave him a few pointers and it was like a whole new player showed up. I love that fire for the game—not every player has it, ya know?"

"Your face lights up talking about this." Monroe smiled as he started to butter his bread. "You obviously really love coaching."

"What?"

"You should think about coaching if…" He examined his bread and then looked at me. "It's an option."

"I'm not settling for a coaching position." Things suddenly felt awkward, and I grabbed my water. Monroe meant well, but hearing alternatives to playing was pretty much saying I didn't have a chance in hell of making it. It was either play ball or… I didn't know exactly.

Sighing, he took a bite of his bread. His eyes shut

and he made a sinful noise that should have been illegal in public. "It's amazing."

I leaned forward. "You totally just had a foodgasm."

His eyes opened, darkening slightly as his pupils dilated, and he took another bite. "Eat your bread, Kalen."

He didn't have to tell me twice.

CHAPTER SIXTEEN

Monroe

Kalen's first date had impressed me beyond my wildest expectations. I'd thought it was just dinner, but then he surprised me by taking my hand and leading me down the street to a wine bar where we painted and I drank wine.

Kalen had been serious about eating better. He was drinking water and at dinner he'd ordered salmon and steamed broccoli. I'd tried not to feel guilty eating buttery lobster and a loaded baked potato.

"This was the perfect date, Kalen." I held my painting carefully as we made our way to his car. "I still don't see what you were saying about my trees looking like penises. Maybe you're just projecting your inner pervert onto my painting."

"You paint vagina flowers as a side hustle. Those are totally penis trees." He popped his trunk so we could lay our canvases flat. "Ah, crap. I have a ton of equipment."

I took his canvas while he moved some of his gear to his back seat. "They're almost dry, we could have just put them back there."

"And mess up my seats? Hell no." He sounded so offended that I had to laugh. "Don't laugh at me. This is my baby."

Placing my canvas next to his, I grabbed his front pocket and pulled him flush against me, putting my lips against his ear. "And if I wanted to defile your back seat sometime?"

"I, uh..." He trembled slightly, and I smiled against the shell of his ear. "I can get a sheet."

I threw my head back and laughed while shoving him away. "You're an idiot. Let's go before I drag you off to a dark corner somewhere."

"That sounds like a threat." He rushed in front of me, opening my door.

I stopped just before dropping into the passenger seat. "It's a promise." I pulled him to me again and brushed my lips against his before climbing in.

He braced himself on the doorframe of the car

and leaned down. "I want you, Monroe." My eyes went to the bulge growing in his pants. "All of you."

"Then get in the car and take me home."

We burst through the door of my house in an explosion of sexual desire and anticipation. I'd been hard for this man since he'd shown up at my door earlier. I wanted him naked. Needed him panting and begging for my cock.

"Monroe," he groaned as I kicked the door shut and pushed him against it. My fingers sank into his hair and I tilted his head to the side as I licked, nipped, and sucked his neck. "Fuck," he whined.

"Yeah, I plan on it," I whispered against his hot skin.

"Bedroom," Kalen grunted, as I cupped his dick and balls through his tight jeans.

Grabbing his hand, I pulled him through the house. Once we were in my room, I shut the door and leaned back against it, eyeing my man. Jesus. That's what he was, wasn't he? He was mine.

"Strip for me, baby," I rasped, crossing my arms and appreciating the view before me.

With a smirk, Kalen began rocking his hips to an imaginary beat and his hands moved to the buttons of his shirt. The veins in his forearms popped and I longed to run my tongue over them. His fingers moved quickly and with skill, the skintight white t-shirt beneath already visible. Spinning around, Kalen let his shirt fall down his arms to the floor, and my mouth watered at the way the cotton fabric stretched over the expanse of his broad shoulders.

"Those jeans hug your ass like a dream," I told him, sucking my bottom lip between my teeth.

He smiled at me over his shoulder and continued to shake his hips, that ass fucking taunting me with every damn move. I couldn't wait to feel him ride my cock.

The shirt went next when he faced me, his hand reaching behind his neck as he tugged it forward and over his head.

Fuck. Me.

Golden abs, perfect nipples, and just the right amount of hair. My eyes drifted down to the rapidly growing bulge that had to be getting uncomfortable. Stepping closer, I reached out and hooked my finger in his waistband, pulling him against me.

"Show me your cock, Kalen," I ordered. "I can see how hard you are... how badly you want this."

His pupils blew out as my words spurred him on, increasing the tension of the moment. "I want you," he whispered breathily.

The corner of my mouth tugged upward. "And

you'll get me as soon as you get that fat cock out and show me what's mine."

"Fuck," he cursed, his fingers fumbling with the button. His earlier finesse and grace was now long gone, he was lost to the anticipation and desire that was rapidly possessing both of us. He pushed his jeans down and his dick jutted out, thick and delicious. I hummed my approval. When he went to wrap his hand around himself though, I tsked.

"Don't even think about it. Tonight, your pleasure is mine. Every moan, every whimper, every shot of lust that bursts through your veins... it's all mine. I'm going to make you feel so damn good," I vowed.

"Please touch me, Monroe. I feel like my balls are going to explode," he pleaded, as he wrapped his arms around my neck.

"I got something for you," I confessed, dropping a quick kiss to his pouty mouth. "Get on the bed."

I made a beeline for my dresser. The new bottle of lube and a small black box were sitting there, just waiting to be put to good use.

"Aren't you going to take your clothes off?" Kalen sprawled out on my bed, looking like he owned it. I'd never had a more beautiful man in it before, and I was going to savor every second.

"Patience," I chided, and lifted a brow as his cock jumped. Interesting. Kalen liked my dominant side.

"Please, Monroe. Please fuck me," he begged, and fire ignited deep inside my body.

"You want me to fuck you, baby? You want to feel me in your ass?" I asked seductively, placing the black box and lube on the bed and beginning to remove my clothes.

"God, yes. I want it so badly, it's been all I could think about the past few days," he admitted.

"Were you thinking about it in class? When I was up there giving my lecture, were you daydreaming about the way I'm going to claim your tight ass?" I dropped my pants, fisting my cock that was already weeping with the evidence of my arousal.

"Yes. I think about you bending me over your desk and having your way with me."

"Good thing I got you this, then." I picked up the box and positioned myself between Kalen's legs.

"What is it?" he asked, curiosity and excitement in his tone.

I removed the lid. "These are butt plugs."

Kalen's eyes widened as I held the smallest one up for him to see.

"I need to prepare you before I can fuck you like you deserve to be fucked. Do you trust me?" I asked, leaning over him with my hands on either side of him, my face right above his.

"Yes," he replied without hesitation, and I could've purred with how good that made me feel.

"Good, that's real good, baby," I praised, reaching between us and grasping his cock. His hips lifted at the contact, and I marveled at how fucking hard he was.

Our lips collided and I slid my tongue against his, my hips settling into his. His cock felt so good against mine, I almost said fuck it to not being inside him.

Almost.

I pulled away, smiling at the heavy-lidded god laying under me. "Just relax into the pillows and focus on how good I'm making you feel." I wrapped my hand around his cock once more and kissed my way down his pecs to his abs.

"You're driving me mad." He squirmed beneath me, and I pressed my hand against his chest to still him.

He groaned as I licked each ab indent, stroking his cock leisurely. My own cock was weeping in anticipation, but I needed to be patient. When I got to the thin line of dark hair pointing me to my destination, I scraped my teeth across his skin.

"Motherfuck—" His hips jacked up off the bed, his dick seeking its home in my mouth.

"Not yet." I ghosted my lips up his shaft, lightly kissing the head of his cock wet with his desire for me.

I sat back on my heels and he practically growled, running a hand down his face. "You'll pay for this."

"Mm." I opened the lube and squirted a generous amount in my hand before grabbing the smallest butt plug.

He watched me, his eyes dark and his bottom lip between his teeth.

"Roll onto your side, baby, and prop your leg up." He complied, and I lay back down, taking him in my mouth. His legs were trembling—in anticipation or nervousness, I wasn't sure. It was a big step to trust someone enough to take you in such a vulnerable way.

His dick popped free of my mouth as I slid my lubed hand between his cheeks. "Tell me if it gets to be too much. It's going to make you feel so full and so, so good."

"Then stop teasing me and do it." He was nearly panting with want as I took him back in my mouth and pressed the plug against his entrance.

With each press of the cool metal, he groaned and his cock jerked. I took him all the way to the back of my throat and hummed as I pushed the toy in.

Kalen's body shuddered and he pushed his ass back, seeking more. I twisted it as I ran my tongue under his cock.

"Monroe! Fuck me, I'm going to come."

Couldn't let that happen—we were just getting started. I pulled away, leaving him panting and thrusting his hips in the air. "Does that feel good?"

"Yesss," he hissed as I twisted the plug again. "Need more."

"Make sure you're relaxed. It's normal if you feel like pushing." I laid my head on his inner thigh and began moving the toy in and out of his tight channel. It was already loosening him up and he'd be ready for the bigger one soon.

"Please," he choked out. "I need to come so bad."

I grabbed the bigger plug and lubed it up. If I did it right, he wouldn't fight the bigger size. I'd never taken so much care prepping someone before, and hoped this would make him love taking me.

"Fuck. Fuuuuck." I'd removed the smaller plug and pressed the new one against his hole. "Oh god, yes, Monroe. Yes!"

It slid in with the slightest bit of resistance. The unhinged sounds coming from Kalen were too much and I gave in, sucking him all the way to the back of my throat and fucking him in earnest with the plug.

His cock jerked in my mouth and then his hot seed was sliding down my throat, his sounds of ecstasy filling the room. I sucked him dry, easing my pace with stretching him. His chest heaved as he sucked in gulps of air.

"That was... fuck. How... what... what just

happened?" Kalen threw a forearm over his eyes. "Is that what a fucking orgasm is supposed to feel like?"

I chuckled, kissing his dick before taking out the plug. "That's only the tip of the iceberg."

I rolled over and reached into my nightstand, pulling out a condom. He was more than ready for me, and my dick ached as I opened the wrapper and slid the condom on.

He was so responsive to me in the bedroom, that I knew we'd be able to explore all kinds of things together. I couldn't wait to tie him up and make him beg for it. Hell, he already was.

"I'm ready." Kalen's glossy eyes met mine and more than just desire was in them.

We were doing this. We were going to fall hard and fast, I could feel it in my soul.

CHAPTER SEVENTEEN

Kalen

Orgasms weren't supposed to take you to a whole new realm of existence, but somehow Monroe had. My entire body still tingled from the cataclysmic explosion that had just happened. If a butt plug could do that, his cock was going to destroy me in the best way possible.

Monroe's face softened as he stared down at me. There was such tenderness in his expression that my heart felt like it skipped a few beats in my chest.

"Lay on your back, Kalen," he purred, as he applied a generous squirt of lube to his cock.

I sucked in a breath as I rolled, my ass cheeks clenching in anticipation. This was like a goddamn sexual awakening. It had burned a bit when he fucked me with those toys, but it didn't last long, and when I relaxed, dear god.

Monroe's cock was hard and his balls heavy as he climbed up between my legs. He ran his fingertips down my stomach, causing my abs to tremble and my breath to hitch. This man. I'd never seen anyone sexier.

"I've wanted to bury my cock in your ass from the minute I laid eyes on you in that bar," Monroe rasped, his voice deep and dripping with lust. A moan slipped from my mouth when he gripped my cock and slowly tugged. "Look at this pretty dick. Your hole is just as pretty, baby. I can't wait to get in there."

My hips lifted as I fucked his hand, somehow becoming hard again already. "Please," I begged. His blue eyes pinned me in place and I quit breathing completely when he gave me a wolfish grin.

"You need me, don't you? Need this cock stretching you, fucking you?" he teased, his hand pulling away from my dick and sliding to the crease of my ass. I pulled my knees up, offering myself to him. At this moment, I'd let him do whatever he wanted so long as he made me come like that again.

"Yes," I shouted as he pushed two fingers in. "Fuck me, fuck me."

He removed his fingers and lined himself up. Leaning over me, his lips found mine as I felt the head of his cock pressing against my hole, seeking entry.

"Let me in, baby. Open for me," Monroe purred, staring into my eyes from just a couple of inches above me. He scanned my face as he applied more pressure and then my body sucked him in. I gasped, my eyes clenching shut.

"No, Kalen. Look at me. I want you to see who's fucking your ass," Monroe demanded, his hips freezing until I complied. My eyes opened and holy shit, it was intense.

Monroe gave me little thrusts, each one giving me more of him, more of this fucking connection that I was becoming addicted to.

"Ah," I grunted when he slid home. My breathing was quick and I felt so full, so stretched, I thought I was going to detonate again.

"That's it, baby. I'm all the way in. How does it feel?" he asked, pushing the hair off my forehead.

"Like the best thing I've ever had," I confessed, my legs wrapping around his hips involuntarily. "I need you to move, Monroe."

He chuckled and that made his cock jerk, which in turn had me moaning like a dick-thirsty deviant. He slid out and then back, repeating the motion slowly for a minute or so before picking up his pace.

"You're so fucking tight," he gritted out, his dark hair damp and hanging across his eyes. His abs rolled and flexed as he fucked me, the veins in his arms popping.

"Harder," I panted. It was getting more and more difficult to form coherent thoughts, let alone actually verbalize them. Monroe started really slamming into me and I couldn't stop moaning.

"Play with your cock," he ordered and I reached down, wrapping my hand around myself and pumping in time with his hips.

"Fuck, fuck, fuck," I chanted. Abruptly, Monroe pulled back, leaving me empty and wanting.

"Hands and knees, baby," he said, slapping my thigh to get me moving. I didn't hesitate, flipping over, I got into position and looked back over my shoulder just in time to see Monroe grab the bottle of lube. "Gonna get you even wetter for me. I want you screaming my name," he growled, squirting the lube right on my ass.

"Give me your cock," I whined. Fuck, I was needy.

A loud smack had me jolting and crying out. He'd spanked me. Holy shit.

Slap.

"Shit," I cursed, my cheek stinging.

"Every time I slap your ass, your hole clenches. I want to feel that around my cock, Kalen," Monroe told me, and then he slid smoothly back inside me.

"Ahh, oh god, oh god," I panted. He was moving

like a beast, his hands gripping my hips so tight I was going to have finger bruises.

Slap.

"Oh my *fuck*!" I shouted. The power behind his spanking increased and with it, I felt my balls lifting closer to my body with each smack.

"Squeeze me, baby."

I dropped down to my forearms, burying my face in the pillow. The slight shift of my hips had his cock hitting at a different angle and suddenly stars exploded behind my eyes, the nerve endings in my body igniting as each slide of his dick stoked the flames higher.

"That's your prostate, you're going to come for me."

"Monroe!" I screamed, as he reached under me and gripped my dick. "I can't, I can't," I pleaded, trying to hold back because I never wanted it to end.

"You can. You will. Come, Kalen."

For the second time, I exploded. My cum shot out, spraying my abs, and I clenched around Monroe, who was still fucking me hard.

"That's it, that's it," he praised, his breathing getting wild.

"Come in my ass, Monroe," I purred, pushing my hips back, meeting him move for move.

With a strangled cry that was going down as the hottest sound I'd ever heard, he came. The look of absolute ecstasy on his handsome face, the intensity of our joining…

I want him. I need this. Consequences be damned.

I was addicted to Monroe Jackson.

I SLEPT LIKE THE DEAD, not moving an inch until the faint sound of *The Thong Song* started to play. Groaning, I rolled over, burying my face against Monroe's chest.

Fuck. Last night had really happened, hadn't it? My ass was a little sore, but the thought of Monroe plowing into me again like that made my balls tingle.

The song started up again and Monroe rubbed his eyes. "What the hell is that?"

"Probably my phone," I muttered against his smooth skin. He tasted delicious, and I wanted to lick every inch of him. "Baker changes his ringtone any chance he gets."

The phone went off a third time and I finally got up, looking around for my pants. Finding them halfway under the bed, I dug my phone out of the pocket and brought it to my ear. "This better be good."

"Dude," Baker whispered. "Where the fuck are you?"

"Huh?" I scratched my stomach and then my eyes widened. "Fuck! I forgot to set my alarm!"

"I told Coach you ate some bad sausage last night and were stuck on the toilet. Hurry your ass up before he makes you run suicides."

I hung up and rushed into the bathroom, quickly jumping in the shower to rinse off. I couldn't go to practice with jizz all over myself, that was for damn sure. As I was washing my chest, I heard the toilet flush, and I looked over to find Monroe watching me.

Maybe I could call Coach and— Wait, what the fuck was I even thinking? I couldn't ditch practice just because I wanted to spend more time with my boyfriend.

Boyfriend.

Oh my god, I have a boyfriend.

I scrubbed my hands over my face and turned off the water, before grabbing what looked like a fresh towel off the rack next to the shower.

"Where are you running off to? Do you want me to make breakfast?" Monroe watched as I dried myself off.

"I have practice." I threw my towel on the counter and went back into the bedroom, looking for my clothes. "Will you help me find my shit?"

Monroe came to stand behind me right as I was

bending over, his erection resting against my crack. "You're already late... What's a few more minutes?"

I groaned and snatched up my boxers. "Aren't you supposed to be the one who cares about punctuality?"

"My dick doesn't care." He chuckled, and his hand cracked across my ass as I started pulling on my clothes. "Do you want to come over for dinner tonight? I'll make you the best pizza outside of Italy."

Buttoning my pants, I turned and hooked an arm around his waist, yanking him to me. He sucked in a breath, his erection evident against my hip. I loved how he was just as affected by me. "I'll bring dessert." I kissed him quickly and let go. "I have to go."

Even though I really didn't want to.

CHAPTER EIGHTEEN

Kalen

Before I knew it, summer was over and fall classes had started, right along with regular practices and training. I'd managed to pass my summer course and felt a new sense of confidence going into the first semester of the year.

I had spent every spare moment with Monroe, even if it was just to take a shower at his place before heading to a study group. Sometimes we'd go days without seeing each other and that was when it became crystal clear to me.

I loved Monroe.

Neither of us has said the words yet, but I was sure he felt the same. When we were apart, he was all

I could think about. Hell, even when we were together and he left the room, my mind was on him.

I guess one good thing had come from not getting picked up by a professional team.

"Dude, did you see all the hot chicks in the crowd today?" Drew, a freshman, asked as we changed in the locker room after our scrimmage.

"Can't say I noticed. I was focused on the game, not the girls." Although, I had found myself seeking out Monroe a few times.

We'd just finished an exhibition for the athletic department's open house. It was a weekend of activities and showcases to bring in donations and to pump up fans and families for the upcoming seasons.

It also meant my mom and dad were here.

My phone buzzed and I grabbed it off my locker shelf before shutting the door and locking it. Making sure Drew wasn't being a nosy fucker, I swiped open the texts from Monroe.

Fuck you're hot in those pants.

I am biting my fist every time you stand and then squat down again. You're going to do that on my dick later.

I'm waiting where you told me to.

I smiled at my phone and sent him a text that I'd be right there. Just as I was sliding my phone in my back pocket, Baker plopped down on the bench next to my locker with a shit eating grin on his face.

"What?" I kicked his leg and squeezed past him.

"Just marveling over how whipped you are." Baker put up his arms and shielded himself as I lunged for him.

"One day the tables will be turned." I punched his arm instead. "Maybe with that chick you've been hooking up with?"

Baker sighed and ran his hand down his face. "Naw, man. She's just a warm body."

"I'll see you later?" I held out my fist and he bumped it.

Exiting out the back of the locker room, I walked down the walkway to where I'd told Monroe to meet me. I needed to see him, even if only for a few minutes before I had to go deal with my father.

A hand reached out and yanked me behind a large brick column. Monroe's mouth was on mine before I could even react. His lips moved down my jaw to my neck as he pressed against me. I shut my eyes and sighed, knowing we didn't have long before I needed to go meet my family.

"When will you be over?" Monroe finally removed his lips from my skin but didn't move away, staying pressed against me.

"Not until late, probably." I rested my head

against the column behind me. "Fuck, I really don't want to go."

"It's only for a few hours. Plus, you'll get to see your mom, right?" He was right, but it didn't stop the bundle of nerves from twisting in my gut.

Half the time would be spent nitpicking over everything about the game. The other half would be spent talking about my training. It was going to be a long afternoon and evening.

"I should get going. I'm glad you came today." I brushed my lips across his, then groaned as his tongue licked at my lips. "Don't tempt me."

"Fine." Monroe gave my ass a squeeze, and took a step back. "We'll finish this later."

Now I was going to have to go meet my parents with a boner. Great.

I adjusted myself and followed a few feet behind Monroe, my eyes on the way his ass looked in his jeans. As if feeling the heat of my stare, he glanced over his shoulder at me and winked.

"Oh, shit! I'm sorry!" Monroe ran right into someone as he got to the corner of the building.

My father.

I stood in horror as Monroe reached out and grabbed my dad's arm before he stumbled into the wall. "Sorry about that, I wasn't looking where I was going," Monroe said, wiping a hand down his face.

"No problem," my dad replied, brushing off his shirt.

Monroe nodded and walked away. My green eyes locked with my father's. I could feel sweat running down my spine and it wasn't due to the heat. Fuck. Had he seen anything?

"Kalen," my dad greeted me as his gaze scanned my face. My heart was racing; I needed to chill the fuck out.

"Dad," I replied and stepped closer, holding my hand out for him to shake. Yeah, we weren't the hugging type.

He clapped my hand with his. "Who was that?"

"Who?" I feigned ignorance.

"That man who ran into me. You were walking out together, were you not?"

"No, I don't know him." The lie tasted bitter on my tongue, and my stomach flipped—not at lying to my dad, but for hiding my relationship. Concealing my feelings for the man I loved. That was fucked up.

Dad's eyes narrowed at me, but he nodded. "Let's go, the barbeque is starting soon and I'm hungry. Your mother is dying to see you. She just returned to the hotel to freshen up. I assume you'll be doing the same?"

"Yes, sir. I need to go home to shower. I'll meet you and Mom there in an hour," I told him, desperate to get away and take a deep breath. I'd already showered but he didn't know that.

"Very well. See you soon," he said, turning and walking away.

Oh fuck. This was going to be harder than I thought.

Baker and I had escaped to my car for a few minutes while I had a minor meltdown about the possibility of my father seeing right through me.

"I don't know, man. It felt like I had a sign flashing on my forehead that said 'I love cock.' He knows, I just know it," I told him. I'd been on edge since that interaction, and felt nauseous as we approached the athletic center.

"There's no way he could know. He didn't see anything, right?"

"I don't know. I don't think so—but the man is like a bloodhound. If I gave off even the smallest amount of weirdness, he will have picked up on it. I guarantee it," I sighed. The whole thing had taken me off guard and I hadn't had time to prepare my emotions.

"Just be cool, dude. You're here with your team, I'll keep an eye out and make sure he's not badgering you. If he is, I'll swoop in and save you," Baker joked, trying to lighten my dark mood.

"Thanks," I mumbled, as we pushed through the doors.

People were milling about—there were small groups scattered throughout the large space, introductions being made to other families. The huge garage door in the back was raised and there were several large grills going, where caterers were preparing everything from burgers to ribs. The food smelled amazing, and I hoped my stomach would settle down so I could enjoy some of it.

"Kalen!"

I turned my head and saw my mom waving with a huge smile on her face. My own smile broke free and I jogged to her, wrapping her in a big hug.

"Mom, I missed you so much," I told her, lifting her off the ground in a tight embrace. She giggled and slapped my chest playfully.

"Put your mother down, Kalen. This isn't a frat party," Dad scolded, and I fought the urge to roll my eyes.

Placing her gently on the ground, I didn't let go of her. I loved my mom. She was sweet and loving. I wasn't sure how any of us kids would've turned out if we hadn't had her.

"I missed you too, sweetie. Great game today," she said proudly, looking up at me.

"Thanks, Mom. I'm glad you could make it."

"We need to talk about your response time. You should've been able to pick off number ten on the other team at least five times in the fifth inning. Your coach should have you do drills for hours over that. You'll never make it to the majors like that." Dad's disappointment was evident.

"Dad, it was a scrimmage," I replied, pulling Mom against me and wrapping an arm around her shoulder.

"With that attitude, you'll really never get anywhere, Kalen. You seem distracted." He seemed to be studying me closely.

"I'm not distracted." Now he was just pissing me off. I was a damn good ball player—it was just never good enough for him.

"Let's get some food," Mom suggested, sensing a fight brewing. I didn't often stand up to my dad, but it was almost always about baseball when I did.

"Yo, Bishop!" Martinez called out, making his way over to us.

"Hey, man," I said as he reached us. "Mom, Dad, you remember Martinez, I'm sure?"

"Yes, hello Jordan. Honey, that triple you hit earlier was beautiful," my mom complimented him.

"Martinez." My dad extended his hand. "Good game."

I scoffed in my head. He never had an issue handing out praise to anyone who wasn't me.

"Thank you, Mr. and Mrs. Bishop. Good to see you guys again. Hope you brought your sunscreen—the Michigan sun doesn't have anything on California heat," Martinez joked, easily making conversation.

"I already put on two layers," Mom chirped.

Martinez turned to me. "Hey, where's Monroe?" he asked, and I felt my face pale.

"Huh?" I replied blankly.

"Monroe. You know, tall, dark hair, professor? Works out with us sometimes?" Martinez bantered and for the love of everything fucked up, I wanted to tape his mouth shut. Granted, he had no idea what was actually going on between myself and Monroe, but I could already feel my Dad's eyes burning me alive.

"Your professor? Why would he be here?" Dad asked, just like I knew he would.

"Oh, well, he and Kalen are friends. He's a cool dude. Great teacher, too. I had some questions about his syllabus, I'll just have to catch him later this week," my friend explained, not picking up on my 'shut the fuck up' vibes.

"That hardly seems appropriate, Kalen," Dad said.

"He hurt his back and I offered to show him some strength training exercises. Nothing inappropriate about it, Dad," I retorted and shot Martinez a look. I knew the exact moment he realized something was going on, because his cheeks reddened.

Looking sheepish now, he grabbed the back of his neck and started backing away. "Right, well, if you see him, let him know I have some questions?"

"Sure thing," I replied. Before either of my parents could open their mouths, I took Mom's hand and pulled her toward the grills. "Let's eat."

We left my dad standing there staring after us, his hands on his hips. Suddenly, I wasn't so hungry anymore.

CHAPTER NINETEEN

Monroe

Kalen had texted me to say he wasn't feeling well and was going to call it a day. I had the sneaking suspicion that being around his dad had something to do with it.

I sat on my couch, my sketchbook open in my lap with a cooking competition playing on the television. There hadn't been much time to sketch lately with the start of the semester and all the time I'd been spending with Kalen.

Kalen.

I knew I was in love with him, but hadn't told him yet. The timing needed to be perfect. I needed to say it soon though. If he didn't feel the same way or at least wasn't headed in that direction, I'd need to be careful. My heart was on the line and I didn't think I could handle a breakup that much further down the road.

Running my thumb along the catcher's mask I'd just sketched, I wondered if Kalen would like the drawing of him out on the field. His eyes lit up when he was playing and I found myself entranced, even though I had no clue what was going on with the game half the time.

My body jerked in surprise as my phone started ringing, dancing around on the coffee table as it buzzed.

The number was unfamiliar, and as much as I wanted to reject it, I swiped to accept the call. "Hello?"

"Monroe?" The voice sounded familiar but I couldn't quite place it. "This is Journey."

"Who?" I didn't know anyone by that name.

"Ah, shit. Sorry. This is Baker. Only the guys usually call me by my last name." He sounded nervous and my stomach dropped straight to the floor.

I put my sketchbook next to me on the couch. "Is something wrong with Kalen?"

"Well… what's your definition of wrong? Because right now he's laying on a hill, moving his arms and legs like he's making a snow angel. He won't get up, man."

"Baaaay! Who are you talking to?" Kalen's words were slurred and then he laughed. "Are you talking to your girlllllfriend? Life would be so much better if I had a girlllllfriend."

"You let him get that drunk?" I wasn't sure what the hell I was doing but I slid on my shoes and grabbed my wallet and keys.

"I'm not his babysitter," Baker sighed. "His dad knows about you, and Kalen's been freaking out since this afternoon. We were drinking but then he wanted to go for a walk. We're in the Arboretum by the administrative building on campus."

"Do you have any idea how much trouble he'll be in if security catches him drunk on campus?" I shut my door and locked it before heading to my car.

It was a short drive to campus, and I parked in the closest spot I could, jogging to the hilly grass area behind the main administrative building. He couldn't have picked a worse building to be drunk near.

As I got closer, I could hear Kalen clear as day, singing in a slurred voice some song he made up about batting for the wrong team. Was this it? Was this the moment he took my heart and stomped all over it?

"Hey." Baker lifted his chin in greeting as I approached, and stood from where he was sitting on the grass. "Maybe we can get him to your car."

"I don't want to go." Kalen was staring up at me, his lips in a pout. "Lay with me. Baker was an old fuddy-duddy and wouldn't."

"Uhh… so that's my cue to leave. I locked his bike up. Good luck, man." Baker clapped me on the shoulder and then disappeared up the hill.

I looked down at Kalen, who was quiet now. "Kalen, what's going on?"

"Hmm?" He sat up, immediately bringing his hands to his head. "Dizzy. Woo!"

He was absolutely hammered, and I needed to get him to my car. "Let's get you back to my place and we can talk in the morning."

I went to grab his arm to help him up and he pulled away. "I'm going to sleep right here. I have to meet my father at six to train. Might as well stay on campus."

He lay back down, and I threw my hands in the air. "Baker said your dad knew about us."

His eyes shut, and I sat down next to him. "Uh-huh. Fucking Martinez had to go and ask where you were."

"And your dad figured it out from that?"

"No, he figured it out when he practically caught us tongue fucking."

"You don't know that," I sighed, running my hand over my face.

Kalen chuckled. "Yeah, yeah, I do know. That's

the thing about my dad. He always fucking knows when something's up. Trust me, he knows."

If his dad knew, that would be a shitty way for Kalen to come out and it probably made me a bit of an asshole for feeling marginally relieved. The sneaking around could end if it was out in the open. Now that he wasn't in my class, it was even better.

"Let me take you home," I said, reaching down to brush his hair off his forehead. He looked up at me. The panic in his eyes was there, but there was also the burning intensity, the way he always looked at me. I loved seeing that look. It told me he still cared about me, despite being worried that his dad knew he was seeing a man.

"Okay, fine," he groaned, pushing himself up to a sitting position. "Oof. Spin city over here."

"Wait a second before trying to stand," I told him while getting up myself. After a beat, I offered my hand and he took it.

"Thanks, Monroe. For everything," Kalen murmured, his thumb stroking my wrist gently.

"You don't need to thank me," I said, pulling my hand away. As much as I'd love to parade across campus while holding his hand, it wasn't the time. Not while he was still a student.

"Take me home, old man," he teased, laughing at his own joke.

"Careful. This old man knows how to handle you," I replied, a brow lifting in silent challenge.

Kalen stepped up, his chest brushing mine. "Yeah," he whispered. "That's what I'm hoping."

With that, he spun and headed to my car, his steps not completely straight but also not too bad considering how plastered he was.

I released a breath and stalked after my boyfriend.

Me: *I got him home in one piece.*

Baker: *Good. Keep an eye on him. His dad is a toxic piece of shit.*

Me: *I noticed. Thanks for calling me earlier.*

I sat my phone on the nightstand. Baker had texted to make sure Kalen was safe and secure. He was a great friend and I was happy Kalen had someone in his corner who was accepting of our relationship.

Kalen was currently snoring beside me. He'd passed out a second after his head hit the pillow. I'd gone through the motions of taking his socks and shorts off, but left his shirt alone, not wanting to wake him. Looking at him now, I couldn't tear my eyes away. His dark lashes fanned across his cheeks, and his soft lips were parted slightly, the pretty pink of his mouth contrasting beautifully with his tanned skin.

I love him. I was in love with Kalen. The past few months had been nothing short of amazing. From going out of town on little day trips to working out and running, we'd spent every spare moment together. I'd cook us dinner and he'd sit at the island, telling me about the new freshmen and how training was going. I looked forward to that routine every day. Watching his face light up as he talked about baseball, the excitement overtaking his features, it was contagious. Honestly, if he never made it to the majors, he'd be an excellent coach.

The few scrimmages I'd been to, it was clear to see that the underclassmen—hell, even the other seniors—looked up to Kalen. They valued his opinion and advice. He was the leader of the team, the heart and soul, with Baker and Martinez his backups. The confidence with which Kalen carried himself on the field was such a turn on for me. He was a cocky bastard, but fuck, it was well-earned.

I turned off the lamp beside the bed and slipped down beside the man who had taken my heart captive. Whatever challenges arose from this situation with his dad, I had no doubt we'd get through them together. Kalen shifted slightly before rolling onto his other side, giving me his back. Perfect. I scooted up behind him and molded my body to his.

The last thing I remembered before falling asleep was him lacing his fingers between mine and holding them against his chest.

"Ugh."

"Feeling rough?" I asked, looking down at the man in my bed. His hair was sticking out in all directions as I handed him a glass of water and two ibuprofen.

"I've had worse," Kalen muttered. "Mostly embarrassed."

I laughed. "No need. I think you were probably at your most embarrassing with Baker. Before I arrived."

"Great, I'll never hear the end of it," he groaned, putting the glass on the nightstand and lying back down.

"Want some breakfast?" I asked.

His eyes were closed again and I thought maybe he'd fallen asleep when he jolted upright. "What time is it?!" he demanded, flinging the blankets off and desperately searching for his phone.

"It's right here," I said, and his alarmed eyes zeroed in on the phone in my hand. He practically ran across the room to get it. "Hey, it's okay. I texted your dad from your phone while you were asleep and told him you were sick."

Kalen's mouth dropped open. "You did what!? Oh no, no. Fuck. He's really going to know something's going on now. Why did he have to come here?"

"You were supposed to meet him at six, babe. It's going on eleven now. There's no way in hell you would've been able to do anything earlier. You were still drunk at six a.m.," I reminded him.

He was pacing, his muscled legs on display. "What did he say?"

"Nothing. But it shows he read it. He hasn't called," I informed him.

"This is bad. I have a bad feeling."

"It'll be okay. Listen, let's get you a shower and some food. You'll feel more human afterward. Your dad thinks you're sick, so you have a get out of jail free card for the rest of your parents' stay." I wrapped my arms around his waist and pulled him against me.

His shoulders shook as he exhaled a deep breath. "I'm sorry. I'm panicking and I—"

"Shh, baby. It's okay. It's a big deal, I understand." I kissed his neck. "Take today and be with me. I've missed you lately, with all of the baseball stuff and my classes. I want to spend the day with you, locked in this house, preferably with your naked ass available for my eyes every possible second."

"Why are you so sexy?" he whispered in my ear.

"I'm even sexier with my dick in your ass," I replied, smirking.

Kalen laughed. An actual, genuine laugh. That's what I was looking for.

"I'm not going to try to argue that... but maybe you should remind me? It's been too long since I've seen such a thing."

"Get in the shower, Kalen," I ordered. His eyes flared with heat, as they always seemed to do when I gave him a command. Stepping back, I let my gaze fall down his body to the bulge in his boxers.

"Sure thing." He grinned cockily. His hand found the back of his shirt and he tugged it off, revealing his mouthwatering abs. His boxers went next with an easy push. I swallowed at the sight of this gorgeous man—*my* gorgeous man. "Be right back," he winked, walking away, toward the bathroom.

Goddamn, that ass.

CHAPTER TWENTY

Kalen

If my head wasn't pounding, I'd have jumped Monroe's bones right then and there. A shower was the best way to try to get myself back together again. I'd had way more than I'd intended the night before, but one drink had just turned into ten.

The truth was, I was scared of losing Monroe. I was a fucking twenty-two-year-old man scared of his father taking away the only thing he cared about, other than baseball.

Twenty-two.

I let the hot water run over my head and down my body, taking with it some of the heaviness that the alcohol had left me with.

I was a grown ass man. So what if my father

knew I was in a relationship with another man? It was none of his business who I loved. He certainly didn't have the best track record—he and my mom didn't act like they'd ever loved each other.

And I could see that now. Now that I was in love.

Turning off the shower, I grabbed a towel and dried off, feeling a little bit better. The smell of something delicious wafted into the bathroom, and I quickly brushed my teeth with the toothbrush Monroe had bought me a few weeks ago.

I can see myself living with this man.

I was going to tell him I loved him. Consequences be damned.

My heart thudded in my ears as I pulled on some shorts and padded out to the kitchen. Monroe was at the stove, jeans riding low on his hips, no shirt and no shoes. He was the fucking picture of my future and I snapped a quick photo on my phone.

"Feeling better?" Monroe looked over his shoulder and smiled. God, that smile was everything and so much more. "I'm making those potatoes you like, and I baked a quiche."

"Yum." I walked behind him and wrapped my arms around his waist, bending a bit to put my chin on his shoulder. "You look like you could be brunch too. Second course?"

"That can be arranged." He set the spatula down

and turned to put his hands on my hips. "Are you all right?"

"More than all right." I brushed my lips across his and moved backward so I was leaning against the island. "If I wasn't so hungry, I'd suggest skipping breakfast."

When was the best time to tell someone you loved them? I knew once I said it there was no going back. My stomach was tight with nerves… or maybe that was from lack of food.

"You need food. It's lunchtime and I bet you barely ate anything last night." He reached up and moved a strand of hair out of my eyes.

I grabbed his hand, moving it to my cheek. "I love you, Monroe."

He seemed to stop breathing as his blue eyes softened and he stroked my cheek with his thumb. "Kalen, I—"

The smoke alarm started going off, causing both of us to nearly shit ourselves. Monroe moved quickly, turning off the stove and then running to the living room to grab a pillow off the couch to fan the smoke detector.

"You really need to get a less sensitive alarm!" My ears felt like they were bleeding, and I turned the range hood over the stove on high. "Nothing's even burning!"

Finally, the alarm stopped and I ran my hand

down my face, my head suddenly pounding and my ears ringing. A cool hand slid across my back and lips brushed across my ear. I shivered at his touch and inwardly cursed for putting myself in such a vulnerable situation.

He was going to tell me it was too soon.

Or that I was too young to know what love was.

Or—

"I love you too, baby." His lips trailed down my neck and across my shoulder. "The smoke alarm just wanted to butt in and tell us how hot we are together."

Chuckling, I moved out of the way so he could finish getting the food ready. "You don't have to say it back if you, uh… if you don't mean it." I slid onto a barstool at the island.

He was so relaxed as he got the quiche and the bacon out of the oven, and started making our plates. "I've been wanting to say it for a while, but didn't want to scare you off."

"I didn't want to scare *you* off." My mouth watered as he set a plate in front of me. "Especially when you cook for me."

He laughed and passed me a glass of water before making his own plate and joining me. It seemed so natural—him moving around the kitchen, us sitting shoulder to shoulder enjoying our meal together.

Jesus, I was turning into mush over him.

THE FAUCET SHUT off in the bathroom while I was sprawled out on Monroe's bed. We'd had a perfect day, just being together. We didn't leave the house, preferring to be wrapped up in each other on the couch. But all of the little caresses and kisses... it was like the sweetest form of foreplay that had gone on all day.

Monroe stepped through the door and froze when his eyes landed on me. Completely naked, my cock hard and begging for attention. I smirked when his hands fisted at his sides. I loved driving this man wild. He was the calmer of the two of us, always in control. It gave me a rush to see him lose his mind.

"Big plans?" he asked, lifting a brow in a move that was so Monroe. His blue eyes practically glowed with desire as he sucked his bottom lip between his teeth.

"I think you can see it's plenty big," I taunted, fisting my cock. Monroe stalked through the room like a predator. He was lithe and sexy, and my mouth watered thinking about sucking him off.

"It is," he murmured, letting the towel around his waist drop to the floor. His gorgeous cock jutted out, the tip already shiny with precum.

I reached out for him, scooting over to the side of the bed. My face was at the perfect height to do what

I craved. Monroe's hand slipped through my hair as my tongue darted out, licking his slit.

"Ah, fuck," he groaned.

"Love this cock." I wrapped my hand around the base and sealed my lips over the fat head. "Mmm," I moaned.

"You suck my cock so pretty, baby," Monroe said, his voice deep and sexy as he began to thrust his hips. I loosened my jaw and let him fuck my mouth.

Over the past couple of months, I'd gotten better at taking him all the way. He went fucking crazy when I deep throated him, saying it was the hottest thing he'd ever seen. One night, I'd even asked him to film it so I could see, and he was right. It was hot as hell.

"Lay back," he whispered. I released him and pressed a quick kiss to the crown, loving the texture of him on my lips. "Greedy." Monroe smiled.

"I love having you in my mouth," I rumbled, not taking my eyes off him.

Monroe climbed on top of me, and I groaned as his hot mouth covered one of my nipples. My hips lifted, seeking friction. The connection we shared with each other was fucking electric.

"Please," I begged.

His face lifted and he stared down at me, our eyes locked together in a vortex of lust and passion.

"I love you, baby." Monroe cupped my cheek as he leaned in and nipped my bottom lip.

"I love you so much," I sighed. His hips shifted and our cocks rubbed together. "Mmmph, so good. I need my boyfriend to fuck me."

He lifted himself off me, leaning over to grab some lube and a condom. I spread my legs and played with my balls as I watched him. Just as he was about to roll the condom on, I grabbed his arm.

"I want to feel you. All of you. No condom," I blurted out.

"Kalen," Monroe spoke my name like a prayer. "Are you sure? I'm clean, I was tested before I moved out here and you're the only person I've been with..."

"Yes, yes, I'm sure. I've been fantasizing about feeling you bare. I got tested last week at my physical. Now please, put your dick in my ass."

He laughed at my demands, but didn't waste time lubing up his fingers. He easily slipped two into my tight hole, both of us sighing at the feeling.

"Love your hole, baby. So perfect for me," Monroe murmured in my ear, driving my arousal through the fucking roof. His mouth landed on my neck as he worked in a third finger and my hips bucked as he fucked and stretched me.

"Fuck yeah, like that," I moaned and shivered as he sucked at the sensitive skin on my throat.

"I want to try something... if you're open to it?" Monroe asked, slowing his motions to lazy circles.

"Anything," I replied immediately.

"I want you."

My eyes popped open. "Want me? You want me to fuck you?"

Monroe bit his lip in an almost shy gesture, and my heart rate picked up. We'd been fucking around for months and he'd never once hinted at wanting to bottom. He told me that the last time he had bottomed had been with his ex, the one who'd broken his heart.

"Maybe we could play with each other a little first? It's been a while..." He trailed off, his eyes gliding down my body to where my cock lay on my stomach.

"I'd love to," I replied, rolling to my side with a smirk. "But I don't want to hurt you. You've said yourself my dick is huge."

He chuckled, kissing me softly before grabbing the lube. I swear he had a never-ending stock of it. "You aren't going to hurt me. Now, get your fingers nice and lubed up. I can't wait to feel them stretch me out so I'm ready to take you."

I grabbed the bottle from him, putting way too much in my hand and dripping it onto the bed. Monroe laughed and grabbed my wrist, guiding me between his spread legs. I knew what to do, but I loved the way he directed me in the bedroom.

He sighed as I rubbed a finger across his tight hole, his eyes fluttering shut. He'd touched me like this plenty of times, but him letting me touch him in such an intimate way made my nerves spike.

"Stick your finger in, baby. You aren't going to hurt me." Monroe rocked his hips and wrapped his fist around my cock, his thumb rubbing over the head just the way I liked.

My lips found his throat as I eased my finger in. He was tight as fuck and my dick wept as I imagined how he'd feel wrapped around my cock. "Fuck, Monroe. My cock isn't going to fit in here."

"Yes it is." He was starting to pant as he pushed back on my finger. "I need more, add another."

I slid in a second. "You don't use a dildo?" As much as he liked to fuck me with one, I had never paused to think what he did when I wasn't around.

"Mmm. No." His hand cupped my balls, rolling them gently, and he gasped as my fingers moved across his prostate. "Do that again."

"Like this?" I hit the spot again.

"Fuck. Yes." Monroe hooked an arm under my knee, opening me up. His fingers were back in my ass before I knew it, working me at the same speed. "I want you to do everything I do."

His pace increased, his hand twisting and

pumping as he fucked my ass, and I mimicked him. With every thrust, he became more relaxed until we were both writhing against each other, our dicks rubbing together between us.

Monroe pulled away from me, and my brain was so blissed out that I hardly processed him pushing me onto my back. "I'm going to ride your cock."

"Oh, fuck." I groaned as he straddled me, sloppily squirting lube on my dick. "Are you sure you're—"

I didn't get the words out before he sank down on me, his head thrown back as my cock disappeared inside him. Both of our groans filled the room as he took me all the way inside him. It was the sexiest fucking thing I'd ever seen.

His tight channel squeezed me like I'd never been squeezed before and my balls were already tightening. I rubbed his thighs, gazing up at the beautiful man above me.

"You fill me up so good, baby." He leaned forward, our kiss bruising as he began rocking on my dick.

He sat back up again, bracing one hand on my abs and the other on my thigh as he moved on top of me. His dick was as hard as stone, bobbing in front of us as he rode me.

"So tight. God Monroe, it feels so good." I rolled my hips to match his as we found a rhythm. "Yes, just like that."

"Mm, does it feel good to have me wrapped

around your cock?" He licked his lips. "Jerk me off, baby."

I cried out as his pace increased, my hand working him hard and fast. "Monroe. Fuck, I'm going to come. Fuuuuuck!"

He squeezed around me so hard, and my balls felt like they exploded in the best possible way. My hot cum detonated inside him as he spilled onto my hand.

"Yes, yes, yes!" Monroe fell forward, his body shaking as I thrust up one last time, his ass milking every last drop from me.

My entire body felt like it had just imploded, and my ears went fuzzy before a light ringing took hold.

I caressed his back and he trembled on top of me, his face buried in my neck. "You all right? I didn't hurt you, did I?"

"It was perfect." His lips ghosted across my neck and he sat up. "Um, I think I got a little too carried away sucking on your neck."

My hand went to it, as if I could feel what he was talking about. "You marked me."

He cringed and slid off me, stumbling off the bed and grabbing the towel he'd dropped. "It's not too bad, but if you have a turtleneck…"

"It's hot outside." I sighed and turned my head to watch him walk to the bathroom, the towel held against his ass.

"Are you going to join me in the shower? I need to clean up," he said, poking his head out of the bathroom.

Monroe standing naked under the water? Yes, please.

CHAPTER TWENTY-ONE

Kalen

I was on cloud nine after spending Sunday with Monroe. Monday morning came too quickly and with it, a pit in the center of my stomach. I needed to go see my parents before they left. They'd come all the way to see me play and spend time with me, and I'd brushed them off. My mom didn't deserve that from me.

After showering at my place and pulling on a high-necked tank and athletic shorts, I hopped on my bike and rode the ten minutes to the hotel. It was the same hotel I'd first hooked up with Monroe in, and I couldn't stop my smile as I walked into the lobby.

"You're late." My father's gruff voice came from the small waiting area near the elevators.

I bit my inner cheek and kept my smile in place. "You're early."

"Sweetie, how are you feeling?" My mom jumped up and rushed to me, pulling me into a hug and then examining my face. "You're pushing yourself too hard."

"Carol, the boy faked being sick. All those years of hard work, thrown out the window, and for what?" He leveled a glare at me.

"I had a really bad headache. Sorry for being human." This needed to wrap up quickly before I punched him in the face. I was so tired of him treating me like shit, when all I ever did was try to please him.

"There were scouts at that game and you fucked up everything!" He cleared his throat and lowered his voice when the people at the front desk looked over at us. "And instead of training yesterday, what did you do instead?"

He came closer and my instinct was to step back, but I clenched my fists instead. "I slept because I had a fucking headache. I'm a grown man. I don't need to explain myself to you. I train hard enough during the week."

Not giving me time to process what he was doing, he reached out and grabbed the neck of my tank, pulling it down. I didn't flinch. I didn't react. What was done was done.

"Who's the girl?" My father's pulse was jumping in his neck at this point, and I was so beyond done with him. I met his eyes dead on.

"There isn't a *girl*." I bit my inner cheek. It felt wrong to say it was Nikki or any other made up woman. Monroe and I were in love, and pretending he didn't exist made me feel sick. What that meant for my baseball career was still uncertain, but I'd deal with that obstacle when it came.

I couldn't keep who I was a secret any longer. Especially not from this man who was supposed to love me unconditionally, but all he'd ever done was make me feel inadequate. Whether I was gay or straight—I'd never get any kind of praise from him. I saw that now. It was like having an out of body experience.

Despite me not coming right out and saying, 'I'm gay,' my father immediately picked up on what I meant. His nostrils flared and his disgust was thick in the air as he released the neck of my shirt. You would've thought my gayness was going to infect him with the way he backed up a step, trying to distance himself from me.

"You aren't a man, Kalen. You're a faggot."

My mom gasped. "Barry."

"I'd rather be a faggot than a bitter old man who's

a bully to his son." I stepped back, shrugging my mom's hand off my arm that had somehow gotten there. "It's time for you to leave."

"How'd he do it, huh? How'd he brainwash you into this shit?" Dad demanded, his voice rising again.

"I have no idea what you're talking about," I hissed, stepping up to him again. Fuck this guy.

A sinister gleam sparkled in his eye and my stomach bottomed out. I wanted to scream and yell, threaten him to stay the fuck away from us… but that would only make it worse.

"I have practice," I bit out.

"Oh yeah? With the softball team?"

Son of a bitch. My fist was curled before I knew it, but it was a small squeak from my mom that stopped me from smashing his face in.

"Kalen," my mom whispered. I took my eyes off my dad for a second to look at her. A tear was sliding down her cheek and I was devastated that I'd done that. I should've known they'd never accept me.

Pain burst through my cheek and I caught myself an inch away from face planting on the marble floors. *He punched me in the goddamn face? Because I'm with a man?*

I could hear staff rushing over to diffuse the situation, and a couple of people helped me back to my feet. Blood dripped down the side of my face, my eyebrow likely split.

"Sir, you're going to need to vacate the premises immediately," the hotel manager told my father.

"Gladly. Carol? We just need the suitcases. Come on, we're leaving."

My mom was outright sobbing now, but I couldn't bring myself to make eye contact with her. She wasn't standing up for me, not that she ever really did before. When my parents disappeared into the elevator, the manager asked me if I wanted them to call the police.

"No. It wasn't the first time," I said softly. "But it's the last."

I COULDN'T BELIEVE he'd fucking decked me in the middle of a hotel lobby. In private? Yeah, I would've been expecting it. Especially after dropping that bomb on him... But publicly assaulting me like that? Not something I could've anticipated.

My head was pounding as I biked back to my house. I didn't have time to apply pressure to my split brow and could still feel blood dripping slowly down my cheek.

But I'd done it. I'd admitted who I was to my parents and more than that, to myself. In the moment, I'd wanted to believe it was because keeping Monroe—the love of my life—a secret, made me sick. And it did, but now that I was removed from the situation, I could see that I'd done it for me. I was tired of being unhappy and since meeting Monroe, I was realizing that I'd been unhappy for a very long time.

Baseball was my passion. I lived for hot sunny days, cleats on my feet and a bat in my hand. The camaraderie with my teammates, the rush of winning—hell, even the disappointment of losing. The sad thing was, I knew now that baseball was the only area in my life that I'd ever felt truly alive. Until now. Now I had a sexy boyfriend who loved me, supported me, pushed me to pursue more than just baseball.

When you find someone like that? Someone who treats you like you're a god, and all they want is to take care of you? Yeah... I was done hiding my man.

I locked my bike up outside and raced up the steps to our door. The world spun as I tried to get my key in the lock, and I blinked several times, gripping the door frame. Fuck, he'd hit me harder than I thought.

The door opened but I didn't trust my body not to go down like a sack of shit if I lifted my forehead from my forearm.

"Bishop? The hell, man? Are you all right?" Baker asked, clearly concerned at my stance and lack of movement.

"Trying to be," I grunted. "Can you help me to my room?"

"Yeah, of course." My best friend reached for me, taking one of my arms and securing it over his shoulders. He sucked in a breath when he got a look at my face. "Kalen, what the fuck happened? Who am I killing?"

"Are we killing people?" Nikki asked, and I groaned.

"When did you get here?" I asked.

"Just now. My spidey senses were tingling," she replied, coming up on my other side to help Baker get me in the house. "Not to mention I got a text from a teammate saying you were biking downtown with blood pouring from your head."

"I wouldn't say it's pouring." I looked down at my shirt and cringed. Head wounds always bled the worst.

"Who did this, Kalen?" she asked, her eyes immediately glimmering with tears.

I took a deep breath to try and calm myself as we began moving toward the stairs.

"My father did," I finally replied. All of our movement ceased. They'd both heard plenty of stories about how much of an asshole my father was, but seeing and hearing were two different things.

"Shit," Baker cursed, shaking his head while

Nikki turned toward the door. "Hey, where are you going?"

Nikki flipped him off. "I'm gonna go kill me a man."

"Oh Jesus," I sighed, wanting to laugh, but afraid of how much it would hurt my head. "Nikki, come back here. I need help. Plus, he's gone. They headed to the airport to go home."

"You're right. Let's get you up to bed, and then I can use your computer to book a flight to go kill me a man—"

Baker laughed deeply at Nikki's threats, but I don't think he realized she was dead ass serious. Vicious was her middle name.

"Come on, killer," I said tiredly. My two friends helped me get to my room quickly.

"So, what happened?" Baker asked, sitting down beside me on the bed.

"What happened was that I bailed on my parents yesterday because I got wasted the night before and then crashed at Monroe's. I just couldn't handle seeing my dad, so I then missed a training with him. When I showed up at their hotel this morning to check in before they went home, my dad had some lovely words for me and then he pulled the neck of my shirt down and found all of these." I paused, tugging the neck of my tank down.

"Holy hell," Nikki whispered.

"He asked who the girl was... and I told him there wasn't a girl. The way I said it let him know exactly what I meant. No going back now, right?"

"Jesus, man. You're so fucking brave. Good for you!" Baker clapped me on the shoulder in a total bro kind of way. I grinned. I had the headache from hell, but I was free.

"When's the wedding and do I have to wear a dress?" Nikki was way too fucking excited about me coming out.

I grabbed a pillow and threw it at her. I'd never actually thought about getting married before, but the image of me in a suit walking down the aisle flitted through my mind. No. We'd both be standing at the altar.

"Man, why did you have to put that image in my head? Way too young to get hitched." I squeezed the bridge of my nose. "I need a nap. Going to have to miss class."

"I'll text Martinez and tell him to take good notes for you." Baker kneeled down, untying my shoes for me and sliding them off. "You should press charges."

"I'm done with him." I lay back, my eyes closing. "I have all the family I need right here."

CHAPTER TWENTY-TWO

Monroe

There was nothing worse than getting a meeting request from the dean's office.

When I had gotten the urgent email after my morning lecture, I had nearly shit myself. It was like being called into the principal's office, only worse. There were a lot of reasons the dean might have called a meeting with me. My evaluation was coming up soon, or a student or their parent might have complained about a grade.

I didn't want to entertain the thought that it might be about my relationship with Kalen. It was difficult not to let my mind go there, though. Things were going so well between the two of us that I kept waiting to wake up from my dream.

We'd been so careful to keep what was between us behind closed doors. Anytime we were out in public, we didn't touch, and if we did, we made damn sure no one was around. But what if we hadn't been careful enough?

Maybe the meeting was about my research proposal. I'd only just submitted it for approval the week before, but there might have been an issue with it, or it had been so jaw-dropping she wanted to applaud my genius.

"Dr. Jackson, Dr. Rodriguez will see you now," the administrative assistant said, pulling me from my thoughts.

I stood, smoothing my shirt and tie before walking into the large office. I'd only met the dean once during my interview, but she was an older woman with an intimidating stare.

"Dr. Rodriguez, you wanted to see me?" I shut the door behind me and headed for a chair in front of her large mahogany desk.

"Good afternoon, Dr. Jackson, it's nice to see you again." She gestured for me to have a seat and dug through a stack of files on her desk, before selecting one. "I'm sure you're wondering why I've called this meeting."

"The email said it was urgent."

She opened the folder in front of her and moved a few papers around, pulling one out. "We received a very concerning phone call first thing this morning that you are engaged in inappropriate behavior with a student."

My vision tunneled, and I was fairly certain my heart stopped. "I'm not—"

She held up her hand. "Now before you continue, the source is very reliable and we have to take all accusations of this nature seriously. Especially when it includes coercing a male athlete in return for a better grade."

"Excuse me?" My hands were shaking and I clasped them in my lap. "My private life has no bearing on my work here at the university."

She took her glasses off and set them on her desk, leaning back in her chair. "Kalen Bishop was in your summer course and earned an overall grade of a B."

Fuck.

"He earned that B. I keep records of all assignments and the scoring rubrics if you'd like to see." Shit, was I going to lose my job over this? My entire livelihood rested in her hands. Ten years of school could be washed down the drain because I let my heart act before my brain.

My heart.

I resisted the urge to rub at my chest. This was bad. If the dean knew, then who else did? It would be all over social media and in the papers. Kalen was going to run for the hills over this.

"As you know, we have policies for a reason, Dr. Jackson. If the student in question were in a different department, it would be a gray area. But he was in your class. Unfortunately, I have to submit this complaint to the Faculty Review Committee and the Student Conduct Review Board for a decision on disciplinary action for you and Mr. Bishop."

I was pretty certain I was going to have a heart attack. "Wait, disciplinary action for him?"

"During his entire tenure here, he has not earned a B in a course unless it was athletics based. Suddenly, he takes a course from a man he's in a relationship with and earns a B? It doesn't look good, Monroe." She almost looked sympathetic.

"What can I do?" Kalen needed that grade so he could play baseball. Was he going to retroactively fail it? "We started seeing each other before he was in my class. He didn't have the option to take it from someone else."

I thought somehow that might help.

"I know what's at stake here. For both of you. I'm not inclined to believe that you would grade your partner differently, but others might not feel the same. What I can tell you is that if this relationship continues, it will give you less of a chance of just getting a slap on the wrist."

"You want me to break up with him?" My eyes burned as I stared at her without blinking.

She frowned. "Is it worth your career? Is it worth his?"

Pinching the bridge of my nose, I tried to calm down and not lose it in front of her. "Did the source say how they knew we were together?"

"Kalen admitted it to this person." She gave me a tight smile that didn't reach her eyes. "I'm not at liberty to tell you who it is, but you should know the man was very irate and used many homophobic slurs in our discussion. When you do talk with Kalen, make sure he knows about the resources we have on campus for our LGBTQ community. I'll be emailing him to schedule a meeting, but wanted to give you the opportunity to talk to him first."

She slid a brochure across to me and closed the folder, but not before I saw a name at the top of the paper.

Barry Bishop.

Where was the best place to break up with someone because their father called and reported you to the school?

The entire way back to my office, I was shaking

and trying to decide what the fuck to do. I had three missed calls from Kalen and my heart sank. He must be a fucking mess if his dad knew and had been an asshole about it.

It was all my fault for practically jumping his bones behind the locker room and for thinking it could ever work between us. Kalen had told me he loved me, but his first love was baseball.

I trudged up the stairs, feeling like complete shit that I was going to have to end things with him. All this time, I'd been worrying about him breaking my heart—I'd never stopped to consider that I would be breaking his.

"Dude! I've looked everywhere for you!" My head snapped up at the sound of Kalen's excited voice, which then lowered seductively. "You're late for your office hours, by the way. I should bend you over your desk and punish you."

I looked around, thankfully seeing no one in the hall and no office doors open. Jesus Christ, what was he doing saying something like that where anyone could hear?

"I had a meeting." I pinched the bridge of my nose as I pulled my keys out of my pocket. "We need to talk."

As soon as the door was open, he went in ahead of me, the left side of his face now clearly visible. I gasped and rushed in after him, shutting the door and locking it.

"Your face." Before I could even ask him if he was okay, his lips were on mine and he was pushing me against the door.

His hands went to my belt buckle and began loosening it. I grabbed his wrists to stop him, turning my head to break the kiss. "What are you doing? I'm at work, we can't."

His brows furrowed in that cute way they did when he was confused. This was going to suck.

"But no one ever shows up to your office hours. We need to celebrate!" When I didn't respond, he backed up, running a hand through his hair. "What's wrong?"

"What's wrong?" I asked incredulously. "You show up at my office with a split eyebrow and what's shaping up to be one hell of a black eye. Who hit you?"

He touched his cheek, like he was just remembering the injury that had to be throbbing like hell. Something was off and it made my stomach twist even more.

"Oh, this?" He shrugged his shoulders, but didn't meet my eyes. "Baseball. What I came here to tell you is that I—"

"We have to break up," I blurted out, needing to

get it over with. My hands fisted behind me, my nails digging into my skin as I watched Kalen's face go from pure excitement to blank nothingness. "We're both facing disciplinary action because someone reported our relationship."

Whatever exciting news he was going to tell me was now forgotten as he stared at me without saying a word.

I cleared my throat, trying to get myself together. "An irate man called the dean this morning and accused me of taking advantage of you." The desire to tell him it was his father was strong, but I held it in. "We have a better chance at us both coming out of this with just a warning if we aren't together."

"You're breaking up with me?" Kalen's voice was calm and quiet, but it didn't keep the pain from seeping through.

I reached for him out of instinct, but he backed up a step. The sight of the man I loved stepping out of my grasp was enough to break me. Kalen ran a hand through his hair again, looking at the ground and then back up at me as he shook his head. "But… I love you and… I thought you loved me."

"Baby, I do." I moved toward him and he put his hands up.

"Don't. Don't call me that." His voice cracked over his words, and my heart cracked right along with it.

"Kalen, it's just… the wrong time. Maybe after you graduate, we can pick back up." But he wasn't really paying attention anymore. He paced my office, not that there was a lot of room. "We're just moving in two different directions. Who knows where you'll be after this school year."

"Is it April? Is this some prank to test my love?" His green eyes had filled with tears, and I reached for him again to no avail.

Fuck. I was going to kill his father for doing this to us.

"The dean will be contacting you about a hearing with the Student Conduct Review Board. I think the best thing we can do is to be honest about our relationship and say we've broken it off." I ran my hand down my face.

"We don't need to—"

"Yes, we do, Kalen! Don't you get it? This is an academic setting and there are rules in place for a reason! If we don't end this, then you'll fail the summer class and I'll be fired! Is that what you want? To not be able to play baseball?"

His jaw clenched. "So, what? You're just going to give up on us that easily? Throw me to the curb after everything? I came out to my fucking family!"

The air left my lungs, my eyes going to the side of his face. "Is that who hit you?"

"Does it matter?" His face reddened and he

turned his back to me, reaching for the door. I grabbed his arm and he wrenched it away from me. "Don't fucking touch me!"

Without another glance in my direction, he stormed out of my office, taking my heart with him.

CHAPTER TWENTY-THREE

Kalen

I threw my baseball up for the hundredth—or maybe it was the thousandth—time, catching it just before it hit me in the face. My life was a fucking mess, but at least I had control over whether I let the baseball hit me.

It had been almost two weeks since I came out. Two weeks since it was all for nothing. Monroe had tried again and again to contact me, but I just couldn't stomach talking to or seeing him again. There were no words to describe the level of hurt I was feeling over his decision to end our relationship. Not only that, but to do it the day after we'd confessed our love for each other, and the very day I came out to my family? Who the fuck does that to a person?

"Hey, you ready to go?"

Baker's question pulled me out of my depressive thoughts. Between him, Nikki, and baseball, I'd somehow kept my head above water. I pushed myself up on my elbows and looked at him. He was dressed in a pair of khaki shorts and a San Francisco Giants jersey.

"Ready to go where?" I asked, eyeing the package he had tucked under his arm.

"Well, my sad little friend... We're going to the ball game!" he boomed, throwing my curtains open with a dramatic flourish.

"Dude. What?" I sputtered. I'd been dying to go to a game but hadn't found the time or desire as of late to make the trip to the Bay Area.

"You didn't think I'd let you forget your birthday, did you? Oh, ye of little faith," he muttered, shaking his head and grinning like a maniac. My lip twitched in response. Baker's energy was contagious. He never had a bad thing to say about anyone, and he lived life like every day could be his last. I could take some lessons from him in that department.

"I— I don't know what to say, man. Thank you. Are you serious? This isn't a joke?"

"Here, go get ready. Put this on," he said, tossing

me the package in his hands. I grinned and ripped the box open, finding my very own Giants jersey.

"Damn, it's awesome. You're awesome," I told him, finally feeling excitement for the first time in weeks.

"Yeah, bro. I know that already. Come on, we have to get going if we want to get there on time. Traffic is a bitch."

"Give me fifteen."

"Man, I will never get used to this level of traffic. It's unnatural. It's an abomination," I complained, as we made our way to the game. The carpool lane was moving along, thank god.

"Yeah, I've lived here my whole life and I'm still not used to it," Baker chuckled, fiddling with the radio. "Are you sure your Michigan ass can handle it?"

I scoffed. "Please. Anything you can do, I can do better," I teased. I was enjoying the banter and the freedom, but fuck if my heart didn't still feel like it was being stabbed every time those blue eyes flashed in my mind. How long would it hurt like this?

My friend picked up on my abrupt mood change when I went quiet. "You could call him, you know," he said gently.

"Yeah, I could. And then what? Get my heart crushed all over again?"

Baker held his hands up in surrender. "It was just a suggestion. I can see how much you miss him."

I did miss him. I missed him so goddamn much that some moments it felt like I couldn't breathe. That if I didn't hear his voice or feel his touch, that my body would completely shut down and I'd wither away to nothing.

"He gave up, Bake. It was our first real challenge as a couple and he bailed on me. He didn't even consider my wishes, he just decided what was going to happen and refused to discuss it with me. I might be young, but I'm a better communicator than that," I bit out. Damn, I was still furious when I thought about it. Initially, I was pitiful. Went back to the house that day and bawled my eyes out for two days straight.

"I hear you, dude. Really..." He trailed off, and I glanced over at him with my eyes narrowed.

"But?" I questioned because I knew it was coming.

"But he knew how much you love the game, Bishop. In a way, what he did—sacrificing his own heart for your dreams? That's the shit romance novels are made of."

I swear, the man was swooning in my passenger seat.

"I don't think I can ever speak to him again," I admitted. "I'm too hurt, too angry... I think I'd worry that he'd leave me like this again and I can't go through that."

"When's the hearing?"

Oh shit. I grabbed my water bottle and took a drink before answering.

"Uh, well... I went yesterday."

Baker turned in his seat. "You what?"

My fingers tapped on the wheel. "Yeah. I couldn't take the waiting anymore so I called and asked if I could get it moved up. I just wanted to get it over with. Monroe wasn't there. I think his appointment is today."

"What the hell, Kalen? I would've gone with you for moral support. What happened?"

"It didn't take long. The whole thing was over in twenty minutes." I wiped my hand on my shorts, my palms were getting sweaty. There was no way to get out of telling him what happened, but I didn't really want to talk about it.

"Why is this like pulling teeth? Just tell me what happened! You're killing me with the suspense."

"Monroe won't be disciplined harshly, if at all," I explained, taking glimpses of my friend to gauge his reaction. Right then, his eyebrows were trying to merge with his hairline and I would have laughed if it had been a lighter moment.

"How the hell is that possible? He's your professor and he had an inappropriate relationship with you, his student. I mean, yeah—you're an adult... But the only way I could see a professor getting off without repercussions would be if the student coerced the professor." He paused, holding his fist to his mouth, and when I remained silent, he sucked in a sharp breath. "No. Tell me you didn't."

When I didn't respond, he slapped the dash. "Damn it, Bishop. Are you trying to sink your entire academic career? Your baseball chances? They'll probably expel you, what in the fuck!?"

"I don't care about school. If I get expelled, so be it. Teaching is his livelihood. If I get kicked out of school, I'll just hit up as many tryouts as I can. I'll still get to play ball. I'm determined to keep playing, but I won't allow the man I lo—" I gritted my teeth. "I won't allow him to be fired and possibly blacklisted from teaching over this."

Baker whistled low and shook his head at me.

"I guess it's true what they say about love turning us into fools," he said, tapping his hand on the console. "All I can say is I hope the two of you get your heads out of your asses before it's too late."

I didn't regret my choice. If I did get kicked out of college—which at this point, I was kind of hoping for—at least I wouldn't have to worry about running into him. I could push my plans for getting to the majors up and I'd have more time to focus on baseball, without having to worry about classes.

"What do you mean, before it's too late?" I asked Baker, who was staring out of the passenger window as car after car flashed by us. We were moving along and the other lanes were at a standstill. Carpool lanes were awesome.

"Just that... I don't know, man. I want that with someone. That connection, the love, the bond. Yeah, we're still young and all that." He shrugged. "You just never know in life. Look at you, you finally figured out who you are. That's amazing; some people never do. I just want an epic love story, okay?" He laughed and I joined him, but I knew he was being serious.

"Never knew you were such a romantic, Baker," I teased, in an attempt to lighten the mood.

"Ha. Then you haven't been paying attention." I glanced over just as he winked at me.

This moment with Baker imprinted itself into my memory; it was one I'd never forget.

A flash of red in front of the car caught my attention, and I slammed my foot as hard as I could on the brake. On one side was the concrete median, on the other were stopped cars, and right in front of us was a red Mustang cutting into our lane.

The smell of burning rubber filled the car and then it sounded like a bomb went off.

The crunch of metal.

Cries of pain.

Glass flying.

My body jerked forward as the airbag exploded in my face.

Darkness.

We never made it to the game.

CHAPTER TWENTY-FOUR

Monroe

I'd never sweated so much in my life. Even after running a damn marathon, my pits weren't leaking like they were as I sat in the hall, waiting for my appointment with the Faculty Review Board.

The heavy wooden door opened and an older man dressed in a sharp business suit stepped out. "Monroe Jackson?"

On shaky legs, I stood and followed him into the room that held a large conference table surrounded by nine men and women. Their stares gave nothing away as I sat at the end of the table.

The man who'd let me in sat down, turning on a tape recorder. "Dr. Jackson, I'm Luis Morales, the university's legal council. I'll be recording this meeting and stepping in as needed. If there are no objections, we can begin."

"No objections," I said, giving a tight smile that I'm sure made me look like a lunatic, given the situation.

I just wanted this over and done with. The last two weeks had been hell. Kalen was ignoring me and anytime I thought about him, my heart broke a little more.

I'd made a rash decision because I'd thought that was what was best for us. For him. But how wrong I'd been. The pain in his eyes the last time I saw him haunted me every moment of every day.

"Our code of conduct explicitly states that romantic relationships between a faculty member and a student that he has, or expects to have, is prohibited. Were you aware that entering into a relationship with your student, Kalen Bishop, was in violation of this policy?"

"Yes."

"We've been informed that to remedy this situation, you ended your relationship with Kalen Bishop. Is that correct?"

"Yes."

The room was silent for over a minute as I waited for what was next. Was this the moment I was fired and blacklisted from ever teaching again?

What the hell was I going to do with the rest of my life?

"This is a difficult situation for us, Dr. Jackson. This student was in your class and earned the highest grade he's ever earned in a course. The sheer fact that he was your student is grounds for termination."

"I understand." I started to push back from the table. If they were going to just fire me without letting me explain anything, there was no point in sticking around.

"However, given the circumstances of the relationship, we will be placing you on probation, pending your formal evaluation by your superior. We are also requesting all student work and grading from the summer course to be reviewed by members of your department."

What?

"Circumstances of the relationship? What did Kalen say?" I was so confused because it was pretty cut and dry. Man meets man. Man fucks man. Man knows he shouldn't fuck man but continues and falls in love with man. Man gets caught.

The lawyer gave a nod to a woman with a laptop, and a recording began to play.

"Kalen, please tell us how you came to be in a relationship with your professor, Monroe Jackson."

"It was the weekend before summer courses

started, and I went to a bar to get drunk. One of my buddies pointed Monroe out to me, telling me he was teaching our summer course. I've never been good at school really, so I decided to be proactive and introduce myself.

"When I slid onto the stool next to him, I didn't even get a chance to tell him I was his student before he was hitting on me. It was clear he was gay, so I went with it. I figured, hell, why not, you know? I knew what the policy was about a relationship between a student and teacher. I'm not stupid.

"Afterward, once he found out I was in his class, he tried to end things, but I was persistent because I fell in love with him. I pursued him relentlessly. Showing up at his office and house, finding out when he went for runs. I convinced him we could keep it a secret. That I would work hard to earn my grade. I assured him the only way he'd lose his job was if he ended things and I told the school, or showed them the video I took of us together.

"So if you're going to punish anyone, let it be me. I manipulated him into something he didn't want. Did it get me a higher grade? Monroe isn't like that. This was purely a relationship built on me needing to have what I wanted, and I wanted him, no matter what I had to do."

I sat back in my chair, my eyes stinging from what I was hearing. Without saying it outright, he had told them he coerced me into staying in a relationship. I knew it wasn't true and my sadness was quickly replaced by anger.

Anger at the stupid policy. At myself for even thinking it was okay. At falling in love when I knew it would end in disaster.

The things he'd said were damning, to say the least. Even if I came forward now and said it was all a lie, they wouldn't believe me. I was the victim in the situation Kalen had constructed.

"What disciplinary action is he facing?" I was surprised I could even speak.

It was silent again for far too long.

"This is unprecedented for the university. We have his statement and if you wish to obtain a copy to press charges, we can get that for you. He will be put up for expulsion as well," the lawyer said.

"I don't wish to press charges." I sat forward in my seat and looked around the table. "Have you ever loved someone so much that it physically hurts to not be with them?"

There were a few nods.

"He told his father he was gay." I looked at the ones that had nodded. "And his father punched him in the face. As you are probably aware, his father is the one that reported our relationship."

"Mr. Jackson, I don't think—" One of the women started to speak, and I held up my hand to stop her.

"His entire life is about baseball. But something else happened this summer. For the first time, Kalen let himself love something else. Someone else." I swiped at a tear that had escaped. "What he said on the recording is pretty damning, I agree. But what's even more damning is that two people... two *adults* can't openly love each other because they fear consequences."

"What are you saying exactly?" The lawyer crossed his arms, a look of disbelief on his face.

"I'm saying that Kalen has already been punched for loving a man, and now he's going to be punched again for loving someone a group of people say he shouldn't be allowed to love. His grade from this summer was his own. He worked hard, and his tests and work show it. I ended the relationship weeks ago, as I was told to do, and he hasn't contacted me once. I hope that you can find it in your hearts to give him another chance." I blew out a heavy breath.

The lawyer tapped his pen on his pad of paper. "I think the review board has all the information they need. Thank you for your time."

I practically ran from the room, and once I was in the hall, I pulled out my phone, dialing Kalen. That bastard had some explaining to do.

The phone went straight to voicemail.

Running as fast as I could, I exited the administration building and sprinted to my car. I needed to tell him how much I loved him and that I was such a fucking idiot for not taking a step back and considering his feelings.

I peeled out of the parking lot, my heart beating so fast my eyeballs were twitching with each thump.

It took me ten minutes to get to Kalen's house.

One minute for me to park and get to the door.

Ten seconds for a crying Martinez to find the words to say, "Monroe, there's been an accident."

One heartbeat for my world to stop.

I PACED in the waiting room, with Martinez and Nikki watching as I lost my shit every time the door opened.

The worst part was not knowing what was wrong with Kalen or Baker. They couldn't tell us much, but what they could tell us was that Baker was in surgery and Kalen wasn't awake yet.

What did that mean? I rubbed the back of my neck, playing what the nurse had said on repeat.

A car that had been stopped in traffic had pulled out in front of Kalen's car which was traveling approximately fifty-five miles per hour in the carpool lane. Kalen had tried to stop, but didn't have enough time. Baker's side of the car took the brunt of the impact and they'd ended up hitting the center divide on Kalen's side. Both men had to be extricated from the vehicle.

I didn't know how long they'd let us stay in the waiting room, but I'd stay all night if I had to. If that meant I'd have to face Kalen's parents when they got here, then so be it.

"Monroe?" The nurse at the front desk was standing up and looking straight at me. She knew me quite well already since I asked her every ten minutes if he'd woken up yet.

"Yes?" My stomach was in knots as I approached the desk, holding onto the edge of it.

"He's awake, but unfortunately he can't see any visitors right now since visiting hours are over." She reached across the desk for my hand, which I freely gave her. "He's very disoriented, so it might be best if you all went home to get some sleep and came back in the morning."

"But… you don't understand." I gripped her hand. "I love him."

"Oh, honey. I know you do. I'll make sure his nurse tells him that you're all here and that you love him." She patted my hand and lowered her voice. "You can go first thing in the morning to room three-sixteen, all right?"

"Yes, ma'am. Thank you. You don't know how much this means to me."

I sat back down, my leg bouncing the entire

fifteen minutes I told myself I'd wait before hunting down room three-sixteen. My stomach had been cramping for hours now and I was thirsty as hell, but I couldn't leave this damn room. What if something happened?

There still was no update regarding Baker. His parents had arrived an hour earlier and were waiting in the surgery waiting room, wherever that was. They'd probably be in there until he got out of surgery. Fuck, I hoped he was going to be okay.

"Hey." Nikki sat down in the chair next to me. I broke my staredown with the hallway doors and met her gaze. "What did the nurse say?"

"Kalen's awake but visiting hours are over. She gave me his room number." My leg kept bouncing. Fuck, I felt like I was going to jump out of my skin.

"That's great!" she said, relief in her voice. "Maybe we should all head back to Alderwood and come back in the morning."

"Absolutely not," I snapped.

"Oh. Well… before Martinez and I head back, do you need anything?" she offered, her voice full of sympathy. I was being such a dick.

"I'm sorry, Nikki." I turned toward her and ran a hand down my face. "I didn't mean to be an asshole. I just can't— Uhmm..." I stopped talking, and my eyes found the ceiling as they filled with tears.

"Oh, I know. I know. Come here," she said, not

letting me say no before I was hauled into her arms. Quite a feat for a tiny woman, but she was determined.

The moment her arms enclosed me, I lost it. We both cried for several minutes as we clung to each other. I knew she was close with Baker too and I couldn't imagine having your two best friends in this situation.

"Kalen and Baker are tough. They're going to be okay. We'll take care of them." It wasn't a question, but a fact.

I nodded in complete agreement, but then remembered I'd just destroyed the first healthy relationship I'd ever had.

"If he wants me," I muttered.

"You're joking, right?" she asked sternly. "That boy is so in love with you."

I shrugged. "I miss him so much," I choked out.

"Then what are you waiting for? Get your ass up and get in there. Kalen is the best kind of man. He's loyal, kind, and patient. He's the type of person you don't let slip through your fingers, not once you have him. Call me if there's any change." Nikki stood, gave my shoulder a squeeze, and headed for the elevator.

I guess it was now or never.

My steps were quiet as I walked through the hall. Nobody was around, which was a relief. I had to see him. When I reached room three-sixteen, I stood before the heavy wooden door. I had no idea what was on the other side. How badly had he been hurt?

Taking a deep breath, I pushed into the room. I didn't see him immediately because of the wall where the bathroom must have been. The beeping of a heart monitor met my ears, along with heavy breathing.

"Kalen?" I whispered. No response. I slipped further into the room and froze. My throat constricted and I felt like I was underwater with the whooshing of my blood in my ears as loud as it was. My beautiful, sweet Kalen...

"Oh god, baby. Oh god..." My knees gave out as I got to the side of his bed and I lifted his hand, pressing my forehead against it as I sobbed onto the sheets.

His face looked like someone had used it as a punching bag. Deep shades of purple, black, and red covered most of his swollen face. One of his eyes looked like it wasn't just shut from sleep, but swollen shut from impact.

His left hand—the one I was holding—looked fine, but his right was wrapped in gauze leading all the way up into his hospital gown.

Bile swirled in my gut and I jumped to my feet, running for the bathroom. He wasn't okay. I wasn't okay.

As I dry heaved, I couldn't help but let a million what-ifs swirl in my brain. What if we'd still been together? What if I'd been driving instead? What if the last thing he'd heard from me was me telling him it was over?

I splashed water on my face and looked at myself in the mirror. I should be the one in that hospital bed dealing with the pain, not him. Not a man who had such a big future ahead of him, but had been willing to give it all up for *me*.

Be strong.

Shutting my eyes and taking a deep breath, I prepared myself to go back into the room and be everything Kalen needed me to be.

Swiping the last of the new tears that had fallen, I walked back to his bedside and pulled a chair next to his bed. "Baby, I'm sorry, so, so sorry."

I kissed his knuckles and rested my head on his bed, exhaustion finally settling deep in my bones.

CHAPTER TWENTY-FIVE

Kalen

My legs burned as I squatted down for the thousandth time. Sweat poured off my forehead and ran down my back, making me yearn to go to the cooler and dump it over my head. Instead, I held my glove in position, signaling between my aching thighs.

The windup, the pitch, the slap of the ball in my glove.

My leg cramped and I cried out, falling back into the dirt, the ball falling from my grasp.

"Damn it, Kalen! Get back up!" My father's angry voice was coming closer as I threw my glove off and clutched my thigh. "Is this the type of man I'm raising? A fucking pussy?"

Instead of checking to see if I was okay, he grabbed the

front of my facemask and yanked me up, my leg buckling under me as I put pressure on it.

"Again." He grabbed the ball I'd dropped and walked back to the pitcher's mound. "Without the mask."

"What?" My vision was swimming with tears from the intense, knotting pain in my thigh. There was no way I could squat with it seized up. We'd been practicing for over an hour after a doubleheader.

"You heard me." He turned around to face me, the repeated smack of the ball into his glove making me want to vomit. "Do I need to come over there and take it off?"

"No, sir." I did as he asked, yanking the helmet off, sweat flying. "But if the ball—"

"Don't let it fucking hit you then." He got in position to pitch the ball and I squatted down, sticking my leg out to the side because there wasn't a chance in hell I was going to bend it.

He pitched again and again. My body protested with each movement, but if I quit now, I didn't want to think of the consequences. He was in a mood, and it was because I'd dropped two catches during my games.

Things went fuzzy around the edges. My reaction times slowed. I couldn't keep track of what signal I'd given.

The ball smashed into my face.

Pain erupted through my whole body as I fell backward but instead of meeting the ground, I landed on something soft, the faint scent of woodsy cologne telling me it was going to be okay.

Beeping penetrated my ears. My whole head—hell, my whole body—radiated with pain. Everything hurt, but especially my face. I tried to open my eyes, but was met with resistance. I couldn't see.

Oh god.

The beeping increased and my breaths came in short bursts, as I tried again and again to open my eyes.

No. No. No.

"Shh." A warm hand stroked my arm. "It's okay, baby. You're in the hospital and it's going to be okay."

Monroe?

I opened my mouth to speak but more pain exploded across my face. An awful, strangled sound filled the room. *Me.*

"You shouldn't be here. Visiting hours are over." I didn't know who was talking, but she moved next to my bed.

"Please don't make me leave." Monroe sounded exhausted and his voice shook slightly.

"Are you family?"

"Yes. He's the love of my life. He needs me here."

Confused by the conversation, I felt myself fading fast, my body growing heavy with sleep instead of pain. A hand took mine and peace washed over me.

ONE EYE OPENED and I sucked in a sharp breath. I didn't know why I couldn't open my other eye, or why I felt like I'd been hit with a thousand baseballs and like I was floating on a cloud at the same time.

I groaned. Ugh. My mouth was parched.

"Do you want some water?"

Monroe? Monroe was here?

"I'll double check with your nurse that it's okay for you to have some. She'll be here in a few minutes."

"Monroe?" I whispered, deciding to keep my eyes closed. If this was a narcotic-induced hallucination, then I didn't want to know the truth.

"I'm here, baby. I'm here," he replied, taking my left hand in his.

"What happened?" My speech was slow and unlike me, but I was too tired to be alarmed.

"You and Baker were on the way to a Giants game. There was an accident," he explained, running his thumb over my hand.

"Baker?" I asked, my eyes opening as far as I could handle.

Before Monroe could answer, a nurse bustled into the room. "Good afternoon, Mr. Bishop. My name is Jane, I'll be your nurse today. How are you feeling?" she asked, setting a large cup of ice water with a bendy straw on my table.

"Sore," I replied.

"On a scale of one to ten, what's your pain level?" She pulled a rolling cart with a computer mounted on the top over from by the door.

"Eight," I answered honestly. I hadn't felt this rough in a very long time.

She typed some things on the keyboard and then checked my IV bag and blood pressure, and listened to my chest.

"I know you're sore. That will probably last for a while. We're giving you pain medication through your IV since you were pretty out of it and needed the rest. We can switch to pills at any time if you'd like—all I'll need to do is call the doctor and get a verbal order."

"This is fine. I'm still tired," I replied. "What are my injuries? Where's Baker?"

"Well, you were very lucky. You have a concussion and whiplash, plus some abrasions and cuts on your arm from the glass that shattered. Your airbag did deploy and you did get quite a bit of bruising from that. From what we can gather, you were in the carpool lane and another car pulled out in front of you from standstill traffic. There wasn't enough time to react. Another car hit your car from behind."

I sucked in a deep breath that hurt my chest. Probably from the seatbelt.

"Where's Baker?" I asked again.

Jane looked across the bed at Monroe.

"I'm not at liberty to discuss any other patient. But if your boyfriend would like to tell you what he knows, there wouldn't be a problem with that." Jane brought the water over and held it up so I could take a drink. "Not too much at first. Let it settle for fifteen minutes or so to see if it stays down. Okay, Kalen. If you need anything else, just press this button right here." She pointed out a red call button on the bedrail.

"Okay. Thanks," I rasped out as I settled back against the pillows. I turned my head carefully; everything spun with the slightest movement. "Monroe. Tell me."

"I want to preface this by saying that what happened wasn't your fault. Not in any way."

Oh god.

"Baker was in surgery for hours once you two got here. His right leg and right arm were mangled. Multiple breaks. It was really bad. He also has some swelling around the brain, so they are keeping him in a medically induced coma until it goes down. They haven't tried to wake him yet and likely won't for several days."

I didn't respond. I couldn't. A coma? His arm and

leg were mangled? His brain? Now I understood why Jane wanted me to take it easy on the water. My stomach was rolling with this news.

"Kalen?" Monroe asked softly.

"I'm tired now," I replied. And I was. I felt like I could sleep for a hundred years... but I also didn't want to talk. I didn't want to think about how my best friend had almost died in a car with me at the wheel.

"Of course," he replied, his voice full of understanding. "Sleep, baby. I'll be here when you wake up."

It wasn't hard to let oblivion claim me.

"I'm Monroe Jackson," Monroe said to someone. I was still half asleep and had no clue what time of day it was, or even what day it was.

"I suspected that," my mom replied, with a heavy sigh. "I'm Carol, it's nice to meet you. Has he woken up?"

Wait. What? My mom was here?

"For a few minutes off and on. He's been in a lot of pain and is pretty out of it." Monroe made a quiet grunt and his voice came from above me instead of next to me. "Um… I'll just step out for a bit."

"Stay. He'd want you to." A cool hand brushed my

hair back from my forehead. "Thank you for calling me. They called Barry and he—" She let out a quiet sob.

"They told me what he said. Did you tell him you were coming?"

"No. Thank you for paying for my ticket, Monroe. You didn't need to do that. I'm sure it'll be any time now that he'll start calling..." Mom choked out as she took a seat on the side of my bed, and rubbed my forearm.

"You're welcome to stay at my house. I have a guest room. No pressure."

"That's very generous. Thank you, honey. I'm waiting to hear back from the bank and credit card companies. If they won't unfreeze my accounts, I'll take you up on your offer."

Unfreeze her accounts? My mother, Carol Bishop, was going to stay at my ex-boyfriend's house? I must have been on morphine.

"Mom?" I whispered, my eye that wasn't swollen finally opening when I tried.

"Oh, sweetheart. Hi. I came as soon as I could. I'm so sorry, Kale. God, I'm sorry for everything." She hugged me as much as she was able to.

"What's happening? What's wrong with your bank?" I braved a glance from my mom's worried expression to Monroe's. Even with just one eye open, I could see the dark circles under his eyes and the wrinkles in his shirt. "How long was I asleep?"

Mom sat down, her fingers finding the ends of mine sticking out of the gauze. I vaguely remembered the nurse saying I had cuts from the glass on my arm.

"Since the last time you woke up, it's been about nine hours. About twenty-four hours since the accident." Monroe made another small groaning sound, wincing as he sat back in his chair.

"Mom. The account?" I might have a concussion and be high on whatever pain meds they were pumping me with, but my mind had latched onto that.

"Let's not talk about that now, all right? We need you to focus on resting and healing." She patted my hand and avoided looking at me.

"Mom," I whispered. My stomach was turning, but not because of the accident. "Where's Dad?"

"He… He wouldn't let me come." She sounded so defeated and I just wanted to, I don't know, hold her or something. But I couldn't. "If Monroe hadn't reached out…"

"You never called me." A tear slipped from my eye and she brushed it away, leaving her hand on my cheek for a moment. "You just… I needed you."

"I know, Kale. And I'm so sorry. Your father, he's… been on the warpath the past few weeks.

Worse than it's ever been and I— I was so scared. He blocked every contact connected to you on all of my accounts, including your sisters, the school, your coach— even the hospital, once they called. He froze my cards... Thankfully, he was at work when Monroe called me. He never knew his phone number."

What the fuck? He wasn't going to let her speak to me? Ever again?

Monroe cleared his throat. "You can stay here with us as long as you need to, Carol."

Us? Did I miss something?

My eye started to close, but I fought to keep it open. There were so many things I needed to say to Monroe, though now wasn't the time. Not when my best friend was fighting for his life and everything had gone to shit.

I'd watched too many movies where the injured person just falls back into the arms of their ex. As tempting as it was, my heart was still a fucking mess over him. He might be by my side now, but how long until he decided I wasn't worth the effort?

I drifted off to sleep, feeling more alone than ever.

CHAPTER TWENTY-SIX

Monroe

Watching someone you loved suffer in a hospital bed was not something I'd wish on my worst enemy. With every movement he made, Kalen was in pain. News about Baker was sparse and anytime Kalen asked, it made his mood even worse.

He'd forced Carol and I to go home to sleep, but we'd returned the second visiting hours started the next day, with high hopes that he'd be released soon. A solid night of sleep had made Kalen more alert, but with that came his anger toward me.

But how mad could he really be after what he'd told the review committee?

"Your mom and I were thinking that once you're discharged, it would be easier for you to stay at my place for a few days until you heal a bit more. She's staying in my guest room, but you can stay in mine." I leaned forward and reached for his hand, which he promptly pulled away, leaving my stomach in knots.

"I want to sleep in my own bed." His eyes didn't move from the television, which had a baseball game on.

"Kale, it might be easier for me to help you with anything. I don't think your roommate wants a stuffy old lady sleeping on the couch," Carol said, patting his knee.

Kalen was probably sick of both of us hovering, but I didn't think either of us could help it. It had been torture being away from him the night before, knowing he was all alone in the hospital.

"Please, just stop." Kalen shut his eyes and sighed.

The door opened and the nurse walked in. "Guess what, Mr. Bishop?"

Kalen sat up with a wince, his eyes glossy with tears. "Did Journey wake up?"

The nurse's smile faltered as she struggled to keep it in place. "Not yet, sweetie. But the good news is that the doctor has signed off on your discharge paperwork. Will your mom and boyfriend be taking you home?"

"Yes, we will," Carol replied before Kalen could answer.

My eyes were locked on Kalen's as the nurse

began going through the motions of unhooking him from the machines and IV. It was like she was unhooking the last lifeline I had to him.

I PULLED my car up to the entrance of the hospital, where Kalen was waiting with his mom and a nurse. Jumping out of the driver's seat, I jogged around to the passenger side, opening up both doors. I wasn't sure which he would prefer, but didn't want to make it more awkward than it already was.

Things had been weird. When he wasn't sleeping, he focused on the television, occasionally saying something to me, but never anything about *us*. I hadn't had it in me to bring up everything and with his mom in and out of the room, it never seemed like a good time.

"I can get in myself," he grumbled, pushing up from the wheelchair they'd wheeled him out in. He'd grumbled about using it, but judging by the pain flashing across his face as he stood, he was still in bad shape.

I reached for his elbow to support him, and he pulled away as I tried to help him the few feet to the car. "Kalen. You're still hurting and there's a curb."

"I'm perfectly capable of walking." He hobbled to

the back door and then looked over his shoulder with a wince. "Mom, you can ride shotgun."

He lowered himself down into the car like he was a hundred-year-old man instead of an athletic twenty-three-year-old. His breaths were heavy and a light sweat broke out on his brow. I wanted to help him swing his legs into the car, but before I could, he bit his lip and did it himself.

Kalen's eyes were shut when Carol and I climbed in.

"You all right, Kalen?" I turned in my seat, the car still in park. "There's something for you on the seat. I know it's a few days late but thought you might want it."

"I saw it, and I'm fine. Let's go." His eyes didn't open and he rested his head back against the headrest.

Turning forward, I took a steadying breath before starting up the car. The doctor had said his moods might be all over the place with his concussion and the pain medicine he was on, but I hadn't expected it to be quite as bad as it was.

As we got closer and closer to town, my stomach flip-flopped. The idea of dropping him off at his house didn't sit well with me. I wanted to be there for him, even if that meant sleeping on the couch so he could sleep in my bed.

Clearing my throat, I met his eyes in the rearview

mirror. Had he been staring at me for a while? I'd been trying to focus on the road, and not think about the battered and bruised man in my back seat.

"I'm a little worried about those stairs at your house. Can I convince you to stay at my place until you're more mobile?" I knew Carol was on board with the idea; we'd talked about it several times already and she'd told Kalen as much.

"Honey, I think it would be a good idea." Carol had been quiet most of the drive, stuck inside her own thoughts about her situation. Her life had been completely uprooted and she still wasn't sure what she was going to do.

"Staying with my ex-boyfriend is not my idea of a good time," Kalen grumbled, turning his head to look out the window.

Carol gave me a tight smile, and I tried to stop my heart from jumping out of my chest. The rest of the drive was silent and over before I knew it.

Grabbing the gift bag out of the back seat, I followed them both into his house just as Carol's phone rang.

"Oh! It's the bank!"

"Answer it. Monroe can babysit me like I'm an incapable toddler." Without looking at me, Kalen started to slowly climb the stairs, leaving me behind.

"Go, sweetie. Remember what the doctor said

about his moods." She patted my arm and brought the phone to her ear. "He'll come around eventually."

I'd explained the entire situation to her, and she'd been nothing but supportive. She said when Kalen loved, he loved with every part of his mind, body, and soul, and that those things needed time to heal from what had happened between us.

How long that would take was still a mystery.

We made it to his room with little fanfare and he sat down on the edge of his bed, his hands clutching the comforter. "I need space, Monroe."

Nodding, I placed the gift bag with his present beside him on the bed. "At least accept this. I know I hurt you and—"

"Please." He brought a hand to his forehead, cradling it. "I can't do this right now."

"When you're ready, you know where to find me." I shoved my hands in my pockets. "I'm not giving up on us, baby. I love you too much."

Before he could stop me, I bent down and kissed his forehead, letting my lips linger. It took every fiber of my being to turn and walk out of the room.

CHAPTER TWENTY-SEVEN

Kalen

"Oh, come on! The kid looks just like you! Look at that nose!" I threw a pillow at the television, annoyed that something so obvious had turned into such a clusterfuck.

My life had devolved into laying on the couch watching afternoon talk shows. It wasn't like there was anything better to do. It had been nearly two weeks since the accident and after staying two nights in the hospital for my concussion, I'd been released with strict guidelines to pretty much do nothing.

Doing nothing was fine by me.

"Hey, man. I'm headed to class." Martinez stopped

at the end of the couch and frowned down at me. "Are you sure you don't want to come?"

"I'm on medical leave until next week. You're going to take good notes, right?" I turned off the television, my eyes starting to hurt from staring at it for too long. Another side effect of the concussion—and a constant reminder that my best friend was still in the hospital and would probably never play baseball again.

All because of me.

"Yes, of course." Martinez smacked my foot. "Baker wouldn't want this."

With a heavy sigh, I sat up and rolled my eyes at him. "I'm recovering."

"Have you talked to Monroe?" he asked carefully. Monroe was a sensitive topic for me. The last time Martinez had brought him up, I'd bitten his head off.

"There's nothing to talk to him about." There was a hell of a lot to talk to him about, but I wasn't ready to hurt any more than I already was.

"Ah, well. I'll catch you later." Martinez left, leaving me thinking about Monroe.

Monroe had been great during everything, even though I'd been a dick. He'd even taken my mom in for a week until she figured out what she was going to do and found a place to stay. He also texted me several times a day, making sure I didn't need anything.

Then there was his gift to me.

After I'd shut him down, he'd left looking like a puppy with his tail tucked between his legs. I'd put off opening it until they were gone, and I was glad I had because I'd curled up in a ball and cried like a baby.

He'd given me a sketchbook with dozens of sketches of me and him. One sketch depicted him handing me a bouquet of his vagina flowers. Martinez had found me hugging it, tears still fresh on my cheeks an hour later.

And I didn't know what to do with that.

By some miracle, I was still enrolled in school, with my consequence being to take a test on the summer course material and to attend all of my allotted university counseling sessions. Whatever Monroe had said to them during his hearing must have been epic, because I was shocked as hell that I hadn't been expelled.

I hardly remembered what I'd even said during my hearing, but I did remember Baker laying into me about it. And I sure as fuck remembered Baker winking at me right before I crashed.

My phone rang, saving me from a spiral of self-loathing. Mr. Baker's number flashed on my screen and I nearly fell off the couch reaching for it. "Hello?"

"Hi, son. He's out of the ICU." He sounded so

relieved I had to control myself from bursting into tears. Baker had woken up a few days ago, but he was still in bad shape and couldn't have visitors besides immediate family.

"Can I come see him?" I pushed to my feet, looking around for where I'd kicked off my shoes.

"Yes. He's been asking for you, but I need to warn you... Journey is different. He might not be in the best of moods when you get here. We're going to head out for a bit to grab a bite to eat if you want to come now and have some alone time with him."

"Yes!" My heart was thumping a million miles an hour. "Thank you, Mr. Baker."

As soon as we hung up, I dialed my mom. She answered on the third ring, her voice lowered to a whisper. "Hello?"

"Mom! Baker can have visitors! Can you take me?" I hated depending on other people for rides, but even if I was cleared to drive, I didn't have a car anymore and even if I did, I didn't want to drive.

"I'm about to go into an interview. Can you wait a few hours? I'm in Sacramento." She was really serious about leaving my dad, which made me incredibly relieved. There hadn't been a word from him, and that was for the best.

"Damn, that's great you have an interview. I'll text you if I can't find a ride. Love you, good luck!" I hung up and scrolled through my contacts.

There weren't a lot of options. Martinez didn't have a car, and I knew Nikki had an exam today. If I called any of my other teammates, they'd want to see Baker too, and I knew he wouldn't want to be fussed over. We were similar that way.

My finger hovered over Monroe's name. I could have just waited until my mom got back to town, but the desperation to see for myself that Baker was awake was overwhelming.

Damn it.

I pressed the call button, knowing he just had office hours this afternoon. He picked up after the first ring. "Kalen, what's wrong?"

Calling him in the middle of the day after refusing to respond to his attempts at conversation over the past few weeks probably would have freaked him out a bit. I didn't even know what to say to him.

"Uh, hi." I cleared my throat. "I was wondering if you weren't busy, whether you could give me a ride to the hospital to see Baker? He's finally able to have visitors."

"Right now?" He sounded like he was moving around, and I tried to picture what he was doing. Was he sitting at his desk, grading? Was there someone in his office getting help on an assignment?

"Can you? Please?"

"Do you want to borrow my car? I have office hours until four."

That was almost an hour until he could drive me. "No… forget it. I'll just call an Uber," I snapped and started to move the phone away to hang up.

"Kalen, wait." His sighed into the phone. "I'll come get you. Give me twenty?"

I took a deep breath, checking my attitude before responding. "Yes. Thank you." I hung the phone up before I said anything I couldn't come back from.

Ugh, I'm such a dick. Since the accident, I'd been a pretty miserable asshole. Problem was, I couldn't seem to snap out of it, despite the self-awareness.

Sighing, I pushed myself off the couch. It was quickly becoming my landing pad and my butt was already bubbly enough. Getting back into shape was going to be a bitch.

I was already dressed so I just grabbed my hat, slipping it on backwards. I decided to wait out on the porch. Anxious didn't begin to cover what I was feeling. I hadn't seen Monroe since the day he'd brought me home. He'd insisted on having me stay at his house, but I couldn't do it. Besides us being over, I couldn't let him see me vulnerable and weak.

Since the accident, I'd been having more dreams —nightmares would be a more appropriate term—of the things my father had put me through when I was a kid. Hell, even as an adult. I was struggling to come to terms with all the bullshit he'd taught me. Which was everything. Being laid up though... it took my mind to a dark place. A man doesn't show pain. A man doesn't get hurt. A man is strong.

But I did get hurt. I was in pain. I wasn't strong at the moment. And I was gay.

If coming out to my family was supposed to make me feel better, it had failed completely. Mom was accepting... now. I was still bitter about things, but I'd talked with my sisters. They actually weren't surprised by my news and were happy for me. It was just the Barry mindfuck I was struggling with.

I dug my phone out of my pocket and pulled up Monroe's text conversation to tell him to forget it. What was I thinking? I couldn't be around him.

A car engine had me looking up, and I grumbled. Monroe parked and hopped out. He was dressed in navy blue slacks and a light blue dress shirt with the sleeves rolled and the top buttons undone. If I had to guess, I'd say his tie was probably tossed on the back seat of his car.

"Hi," he said, coming to a stop at the porch.

"Hey," I replied, slipping my hands into my pockets.

It was awkward. Really fucking awkward.

"You ready to go?" Monroe asked, shifting from foot to foot.

"Yeah. Let's do it," I said, stepping down and

speed walking past him to the car. I underestimated how much it would take out of me, and I sucked in a breath when a pain shot through my chest, my body protesting the speed at which I was walking.

"Hey, hey, slow down. Are you okay? Do you need help?" he asked, running up behind me as I stopped to take a few deep breaths.

"No. I don't need any help. I need to get to the hospital to see my best friend who I almost killed," I gritted out between clenched teeth.

Monroe stepped back, his eyes wide. "Okay," he said after a moment, leaving my stubborn ass standing there as he got into his car.

The drive over was full of music and tension. I knew he wanted to say something—hell, probably a lot of things. The way his hand gripped the steering wheel made the veins in his arm pop out, but he didn't speak. I wasn't sure if I was relieved or devastated. My mood swings were so unstable, another complication of a concussion. How long was I going to be fucked up?

Baker will probably be fucked up for a long time...

"Do you want me to come in with you?" Monroe asked as we pulled into the hospital parking lot.

"No," I replied immediately. "But thank you for offering."

"How are you getting home?" he asked, pulling up to the drop off entrance.

"I don't know. Hopefully, he's okay with me hanging out for a while. Visiting hours are over at seven. Do you think you could come back and get me then?" I asked him, taking care not to make eye contact. I couldn't look him in the eyes. Not now. They'd probably be full of pity. Or anger.

"Sure. I'll pick you up from this entrance in a couple of hours. Tell Baker I said hello and I hope his recovery is going well."

I carefully got out of the car. "I'll tell him. Thanks for the ride."

With that, I closed the door and shuffled toward the entrance.

Before I knew it, I was standing in front of room four hundred twenty. Baker's parents caught me just as I arrived as they were on their way out to get dinner. They both warned me that he wasn't in a good mood. But that made two of us, so we could be grumpy assholes together. If he'd been asking for me, I guess that meant he still wanted to be friends.

I pushed through the door and immediately our eyes connected. Baker's head was wrapped in gauze, his leg in a cast up to his hip and his arm casted up to his armpit.

"Jesus," I whispered before I could stop myself.

"No, just me. Your old pal, Baker," he replied.

"Baker... I'm so—"

"Don't," he bit out. His eyes darted to the door. "Where's Monroe?"

"What do you mean, where's Monroe?" I approached his bed cautiously, not quite sure how to act around him. He seemed to be the same old Baker but his eyes weren't as bright as they usually were and his smile was nonexistent. "We broke up, you don't remember?"

Wrong. Thing. To. Say.

His face flushed, and the fist of his unbroken arm clutched the blanket so hard, I thought he might rip a hole in it. I was such an idiot for asking him that. Hell, he'd been in a fucking coma.

"You haven't even said anything about how amazing my face looks." I gestured to it to distract him from his anger. "I think yellow looks good on me."

"Yeah. Yeah, it does." He shut his eyes, taking deep breaths, and kept them closed. "Fuck, man."

Sitting down in the chair next to his bed, I looked at him. Really looked at him. His face had the last remnants of bruising like mine did, and there was a giant cut above his eye. I didn't even want to know what was under the bandage on his head. Had they had to crack his skull to relieve the pressure?

Before I knew it, tears were sliding down my cheeks. We'd almost fucking died.

"Don't, Kalen." Baker unfisted the blanket and

reached for my hand. I took it immediately, squeezing so tightly he winced. "There have been so many tears cried in that damn chair that there's now a fucking moat around this bed."

I snorted and wiped my cheeks with my free hand, meeting his chestnut eyes. "How are you doing?"

"Well, I'm stuck in this damn hospital bed for at least another few days before they move me to a rehabilitation place for a few weeks." He squeezed my hand. "But I'm alive, right?"

"I'm so sorry, maybe if—"

"I'm going to kick you out if you keep that shit up. It wasn't your fault and the last thing I need is for my best friend to be acting weird around me when everyone else already treats me like I'm a delicate flower." His eyes fluttered closed, and he groaned in pain.

Panic took hold and blood rushed to my ears. "What's wrong? Do you need me to get the nurse?" I scooted to the very edge of my chair.

"No. Just. Need. A. Second," he gritted out.

He let go of my hand and grabbed a button, pressing it down as hard as he could. He let it go, seeking out my hand again, his eyes still closed in pain. I hated seeing him like this. It should be me in his place.

"I can't imagine the pain you must be in. I just

stopped my pain pills the other day and I'm feeling it," I whispered, hoping my words helped distract him instead of making it worse.

Silence fell between us, and I wondered if he'd changed his mind about blaming me or if he'd fallen asleep. His breaths evened out and I relaxed back into my chair, his hand still in mine.

I was just about to shut my eyes and take my own little nap when he squeezed my hand. "Why haven't you kissed and made up with Monroe?" His voice was barely audible, his eyes still shut.

I leaned forward, putting my forehead on the railing of his bed, the cool metal soothing the ache that was starting to bloom there. "I don't know... I'm moody as fuck right now."

"Me too." Baker sniffled, and I lifted my head to find him crying with his eyes shut. "I'm so scared. Sometimes I can't remember something and I search for it and it's gone..."

I opened my mouth to say I was sorry, but he continued before I could.

"What you and Monroe have? Don't let that slip away just because you're a stubborn bastard. Let him back in. Let him love you the way you deserve to be loved." He bit his lip. "It would be so much easier if I had someone like that."

"You have me." I stood, not letting go of his hand, and reached for a tissue on his hospital table. I dabbed at his cheeks. A small smile quirked up the corners of his mouth, and his eyes opened a sliver. "What?"

"You wouldn't wipe my ass, would you?"

I cringed. "Ew. What?"

"You'd wipe Monroe's though." His eyes closed again. "That's how you know he's your forever."

"Dude." I chuckled. "That's some deep shit."

He laughed and then groaned. "Ow. Don't be funny."

"You're the one that started talking about wiping asses." I plopped down. "I know this is going to sound weird, but I'm starting to feel like maybe I should say it more often to the people I care about… I love you. I'm so lucky to have you in my life."

Baker smiled, a genuine smile, which looked a little creepy with his eyes closed. "I love you too, man." His head nodded to the side, his smile slowly fading as he drifted off to sleep.

As I watched him, I couldn't stop thinking about my own words. I should say it more often to the people I cared about.

Monroe.

CHAPTER TWENTY-EIGHT

Monroe

From the moment I picked up Kalen's call, my stomach had been in knots. It had been a rough few weeks, wondering when or if he was going to give me another chance. A chance at showing him how much I loved and cared for him.

Maybe it had been wishful thinking, but the whole time I was at the hospital with him, I'd started to believe that everything would be okay.

How wrong I was.

As the time on the clock drew closer and closer to seven, I wondered if this was it for us. I couldn't keep losing sleep and giving myself an ulcer. I loved him with every fiber of my being, but he didn't seem to love me at all anymore.

I put my head on the steering wheel, taking deep breaths to calm my nerves. He hated me and I didn't know how to undo the damage I'd caused.

My phone rang and I jumped, quickly grabbing it from my cupholder and bringing it to my ear. "Kalen?"

"Hey." He sounded distant, like he didn't even have the phone near his mouth. "I'm ready to go."

"I'll be right there. I'm in the parking lot." Hanging up, I started my car and backed out of the parking space. I could do this. I had the strength to sit in the car with him for the thirty-minute drive back.

Pulling up to the curb where he was standing, I tried to get a read on him. His face was blank and he got into the passenger seat quickly, buckling his belt and taking hold of the door handle.

I wanted to ask him how Baker was doing, how *he* was doing, but his clenched jaw stopped me. It seemed we were going to ride back in the same silence as we'd come in.

About fifteen minutes into the drive, he whispered, "Pull over."

"What?" I glanced at him briefly, his face hidden as he stared out the side window. "Here?"

"Up here. Pull off." His voice shook. "Please. I can't be in this car anymore."

My heart hurt at his words, but I did as he asked

and took the next exit, which had a few convenience stores and fast food places on one side, and a field on the other. I got far enough away from the highway exit before pulling onto the dirt shoulder next to the field. As soon as I put the car in park, he threw his door open and jumped out.

The road we were on wasn't a busy one, thankfully. I hopped out of the car, my heart pounding as I watched Kalen pace back and forth in a tomato field. His face was getting redder by the second, and I wasn't prepared for the absolute explosion that happened.

"What's your angle here, Monroe? You take my mom in, you give me a ride when I was nothing but a dick to you... What are you doing?" he shouted.

My mouth fell open. Was he serious right now?

"You want to do this here? Now?" I asked calmly.

He threw his arms up in the air. "Well, why the hell not? Seems like as good a time as any!"

"I took your mother in because she had nowhere to go. No money. And I know that despite what happened in your past, you love her. You're both victims of your father's abuse," I explained to him, unbuttoning my dress shirt because it was hot as hell.

"And you did that out of the kindness of your heart?" he seethed. He was livid. Absolutely furious, his eyes glittering with anger and rage... But beneath that, the pain I'd caused him was there.

"Kalen, I don't want to fight with you." I slipped my shirt off and tossed it on the car. My white t-shirt felt so much better.

He started pacing again, and I wished he'd just settle the fuck down.

"I think maybe you should get back in the car," I told him, worried that he was going to get himself really worked up. Carol had told me he was still having headaches and wasn't supposed to be doing much, in order to give his brain a rest. Seeing Baker had to have been one hell of a shock.

"And I think you don't get to say things like that anymore," he tossed back.

"You're acting like a child."

He froze and slowly looked over at me. I was leaning up against the passenger side of the car now.

"Ah, there we have it." He laughed, without a trace of humor.

I ground my teeth so hard, my jaw ached. "What the fuck is that supposed to mean?"

"You never wanted to be serious with me. Right? I'm too young? A convenient reason to end things later when it was getting too real. You had me fooled for a while, though."

I saw red. He thought I was just using him as a hole to fuck?

"Are you fucking kidding me?" I roared. There was no stopping it. I was pissed now and if that was his goal, he'd succeeded. "I sacrificed everything for you. For a relationship. With. You!"

"Yeah? Well, in the end, you weren't really willing to sacrifice it though, were you?"

"I fucked up. I've regretted it every second since. And then you tried to throw your academic career down the drain! Why would you do that?" I ran my hands through my hair, really wanting to rip it out.

"BECAUSE I LOVE YOU!" he boomed, bending down and scooping something up off the ground. Before I could react, a tomato exploded on my chest.

He'd thrown a tomato at me. My college baseball all-star ex-boyfriend had just thrown a goddamn tomato at me. I was frozen, staring down at the seeds and chunks of tomato dripping down my shirt. It looked like my heart had just exploded.

"Why did you leave me, Monroe!? WHY? How could you do that to me?" I glanced up just in time to see him hit the ground. Tears clouded my vision now and I could barely see as I stumbled away from the car, toward the broken man I loved.

He had another tomato clenched in his fist as he cried.

"Kalen, I fucked this up. Me. I did this to us." My voice cracked as I lowered myself in front of him. I had to get through to him. I might not get another chance. "Please, look at me." His watery eyes slammed into mine and I swallowed roughly.

"I love you so much it hurts. It hurts me every moment you're not with me. Even when we were together, every day that went by and I didn't get to see you? You were all I could think about. That day in my office, I wanted to take back the words I said the second they came out of my mouth, but the damage was already done. I did what I did because I thought you could still have a shot at your baseball dreams if I discreetly stepped away." I reached for his hands and when he didn't yank them away, I slowly removed the bruised tomato from his grip.

"If I thought the two weeks that went by while I waited for that hearing were hell? I swear to god, when I found out you'd been in a serious car accident? I'd just finished my own hearing and discovered what you'd done. I was furious and I went to your house to confront you. That's when Martinez told me... I've never known fear like that in my life."

I watched as a tear raced down his cheek and fell to the dusty ground.

"You destroyed me," he whispered. "I came out to my parents, thinking I had a serious relationship that was going to last. I saw forever, Monroe. I've never had that happen before. And then you were gone. I saw forever!"

My chest may as well have been flayed open for

the vultures to descend upon, because the passion, the hurt... It was as though his words had cracked my sternum and the betrayal he felt was squeezing the life out of me.

"I love you, Kalen. We can fix this. I know we can. Let me show you. I want forever, baby. You and me, always," I blurted out. It was so unlike me, but Jesus, I was desperate. I felt like I was losing him with each second, and I didn't know how to live without him in my life.

His eyes shut. "Can you just take me home?"

Without a word, I stood, looking down at him. I couldn't just take him home, not like this. Not when there were so many things left unsaid and he was an emotional mess. If I let him close the door on me now, I'd probably never get him to open it again.

He stood, wiping his hands on his shorts and kicking at the tomato I'd taken from him. "I threw a tomato at you."

My fingers itched to cup his cheek, to run my thumb across his lips, but instead I grabbed the front of my shirt, pulling it away from my body to examine the remnants of the tomato assault. "I deserved it. Come on." I walked back to the car, rounding the front and grabbing my discarded dress shirt. "Are you hungry?"

Kalen had followed a few feet behind me and opened the passenger door. "No."

I blew out a shaky breath as he lowered into the car. It was like a switch had been flipped, and he had gone from wanting to peg me with tomatoes to silence. I didn't know which was worse. At least with him yelling at me, I was getting something out of him, instead of the silence that made my blood turn to ice.

Opening the driver's door, I leaned in and grabbed my tumbler of water. The tomato juice had seeped through my shirt, making me feel sticky and gross. I pulled my shirt over my head and tossed it in the back seat with my dress shirt, before pouring the water on my chest.

"You've got to be kidding me right now," Kalen muttered.

"What?" I lowered myself into the car, my chest dripping, and turned it on.

"You just... ripped your shirt off and poured water down your chest." He buckled his seatbelt. "I see what you're trying to do, Monroe."

"What is it you think I'm trying to do, Kalen? My chest was sticky from the tomato. Would you have preferred if I asked you to lick it clean for me?" I buckled my own seatbelt and looked over at him. He was staring out the side window. "Come home with me."

When he didn't respond, I put the car in drive and pulled back onto the road. It wasn't long until we were back in Alderwood, and I took the farthest exit from Kalen's place, hopeful in the extra time it took that he'd change his mind.

His phone rang and he dug it out of his pocket, swiping it and bringing it to his ear. "What's up?... That's great... Yeah, I saw him... I don't really want to talk about it... I'm fine... Love you too." He hung up.

Before I could even open my mouth to ask him if it had been his mom just so that there was some small talk, my phone rang, Carol's name flashing on the dash display.

"Hi, Carol."

"I got the job! I just wanted to thank you again for practicing interviewing with me. It really helped. It had been a long time since I had to do it."

"Anytime. I'm so excited things are coming together for you. We should go out and celebrate soon."

"Oh, I'm too old for that." She laughed and then sighed. "Have you heard from Kalen? He went to see Baker today and I'm worried about him."

"He'll talk to me when he's ready." I braved a glance over at Kalen and then focused on driving. "I broke his heart, I don't know if he'll ever forgive me."

"He's a stubborn boy. Give him time—he'll come around. Hopefully not before it's too late. If I've learned anything over the past few weeks it's that love isn't just in the words you say but the actions you take. And you, my dear, love harder than anyone I've ever met." She sniffled. "I'll let you go. Take care!"

"You too, Carol." We hung up and the radio switched back on, but I wasn't in the mood for music.

I reached forward to turn it off, and Kalen grabbed my wrist, sliding his hand into mine. "Thank you for taking care of my mom when I couldn't." He rested our hands on the center console, not letting go. "I'm a little hungry."

His stomach growled at that same moment, and we both laughed at the timing. My heart was beating so hard, I was sure he could feel it.

"We can grab burgers, and I can drop you off at your place." I didn't want to push my luck.

He was holding my hand and in that moment, there was no better feeling in the world.

CHAPTER TWENTY-NINE

Kalen

We pulled up to my house after grabbing dinner from the drive-thru. Part of me was disappointed he didn't just ignore me and take me to his place. I'd finally calmed my ass down after completely losing it. It had been bubbling under the surface for weeks, and now I just felt... sad.

Sad that Baker was struggling and didn't know what his future was going to look like now.

Sad that my mom had given up her entire life, even if that life had been fucked up.

And the worst sadness was that I'd completely lost it on the man sitting next to me, who had broken my heart yet now wanted to put it back together again. He loved me and I loved him, so why was I being such a dick?

"I should have asked for separate bags." Monroe reached into the back seat and grabbed the food. He started to open it and I put my hand over his. "What?"

"That's how you know he's your forever." Baker's words echoed in my head.

"I'd wipe your ass if you needed me to," I said with certainty. His face displayed about one hundred different emotions at once. "And you'd wipe mine."

"Well, umm... sure?" His brows furrowed in confusion. "Is that something you're struggling with from the accident? Your mom didn't tell me—"

Grabbing the back of his neck, I pulled him halfway over the console and kissed him. He gasped, opening his mouth to me and letting my tongue in. It had been so long since I'd kissed him and I didn't ever want that to happen again.

His fist tightened on the bag of food and I pulled back, putting my forehead against his. "I love you, Monroe."

"Baby," he breathed. "I love you so goddamn much." His lips pressed against mine gently, like he was savoring every second. Sweet, small kisses between us were the stepping stones to mending what was broken and I could've kicked my own ass for going so long without.

"Can I still come over?" I whispered against his mouth. Monroe pulled back, his blue eyes swirling with love, heat, and hope.

"Put your seatbelt on, Kalen," he rasped in that sexy, domineering voice he liked to use to drive me wild.

I kissed him once more, before sitting back in the seat and buckling myself in. He put the car in drive and reached across the console, letting his hand land high on my thigh. My heart swelled at the possessive touch. Baker was right. I had a man who loved me, a man who was willing to do whatever he could to make sure I was happy. The way he'd been there for my mom alone... I could never repay him.

We didn't speak as we made the drive to his house, but it wasn't like before. This silence was charged with tension of a different kind. When we arrived, Monroe grabbed our drinks, his shirt, and tie while I carried the food. My eyes were glued to his ass as he walked in front of me. Dress slacks on this man should be a crime. How could anyone think they were professional when his ass looked like that? And he was still shirtless. *Shirtless.*

"Are you checking me out?" he teased, as he unlocked the door.

"Absolutely," I replied with a grin.

God, it felt so good to smile. It felt even better to let go of all the bullshit and just be with him.

I followed him to the kitchen where he set our drinks on the island. "Let me grab some plates," he said, turning to get them from the cabinet but I was right there, blocking him. Reaching out, I trailed my hand down his chest, loving the way his breathing hitched at my touch.

"Fuck," I sighed. "I missed you."

He growled and his large hands landed on my ass, pulling me against him. Our cocks pressed against each other and I groaned. Monroe's mouth moved from my lips to my jaw, making his way down my throat. When he bit my collarbone, I thought I was going to die.

"Need you," he said, his voice thick with desire.

My hands sank into his hair and I pulled his head up to look him in the eyes. His tongue snaked out, wetting his bottom lip and I tracked the movement like a predator.

"Take me."

Monroe's pupils dilated, nearly eclipsing the blue of his iris. His hands pulled up my t-shirt, dragging it over my head before he tossed it behind him. I furiously worked his belt buckle, while he slid my shorts and boxers over my hips. I fumbled with his button in my haste to get him naked, but it was brief. His cock slapped his stomach as it sprang free from the confines of his boxers and I groaned.

"Oh god," I whispered. "So fucking sexy." I started to drop to my knees, but he halted me.

"When I make you mine again, it's going to be in my bed."

Holy shit. I didn't know how this man had the ability to turn me to mush with his filthy words, but I never wanted to stop hearing them. His hand slipped into mine and he led me to his room.

We were a clash of skin, sweat, and fire.

I couldn't stop touching him, like if I stopped he'd disappear and I'd never have this feeling again. The intensity, the fucking passion... I'd already gone without it for too long and I was a shell of the man I'd been when I was his.

He pushed me on the bed and crawled on top of me, kissing my mouth and neck before working his way to my chest, nipples, and abs.

"Monroe," I breathed when he licked my hip bone. "I want to taste you." I somehow got the words out despite my head spinning from all of the sensations, or maybe it was that mixed with the lingering effects of the concussion. Regardless, the man was making me wild.

"Mmm, I know," he replied, his warm breath against my cock serving as another form of sweet torture. "Later."

The first swipe of his tongue over the slit of my dick had me crying out and fisting the sheets. When he sucked my length into his mouth and bobbed his head, I could have shed more tears if I'd had any left. But I was tired of crying. I needed him. My hips lifted in time with the pace he'd set.

"That's it, baby. Fuck my face with that pretty dick," he growled before diving back down, swallowing me whole.

"Oh fuck, babe. God. Yes. Like that, like that. I'm gonna come, ahhh."

"Give it to me," he demanded, slurping my cock down like a starved man. With a full body shudder, my muscles clenched and I fired rope after rope of hot cum down my man's throat. He greedily sucked, ensuring all of it was his.

Monroe popped my dick out of his mouth, and our gazes connected as he wiped the corner of his lips with two fingers and licked them clean.

"Come here," I panted, still feeling the aftershocks of my orgasm. He lowered himself on his forearms, hovering above my face. "Kiss me, Monroe."

As we kissed, I reached between us, seeking his cock.

"Mmm, yes, like that," he purred. His hips rocked as he fucked my hand.

I pulled him down, whispering in his ear. "Need to taste you. Put that dick in my mouth."

"Stay right there," he warned, as he walked on his knees up my body and then leaned over. His thick length was right where I wanted it and I gripped his hips and surged up, wrapping my lips around him.

"Fuuuuck," he moaned. "Yes, like that, baby. Take me."

I was picturing him pounding my ass the same way he was my mouth. My cock was already hardening again.

"Kalen, I need to be inside of you." His movements faltered and I released him.

"Good, because I need you inside of me. Now."

Monroe fumbled with the nightstand, grabbing a bottle of lube and a butt plug.

"A plug? I don't want a plug, I want your cock."

He chuckled. "The plug is for me, baby. I want you to put it in me so I can clench around it while I fuck you."

"Holy hell, Monroe. You kinky bastard," I joked, sitting up now and grabbing the small plug.

He laid down on the bed, spreading his legs while I positioned myself between them. I put a generous amount of lube on the toy and pressed my slicked up fingers to his hole. He immediately clenched, giving me visions of the night he rode my cock.

I slipped a finger in, quickly working my way up to a second. "Put it in me, baby. I can't wait anymore."

Using the tip of the plug, I fucked him, captivated by how hot it was to see his hole stretched.

"Fuck, fuck," he cursed, when the largest portion of the plug breeched his body.

"You okay?" I asked, needing to make sure he wasn't hurt.

A slow grin was his only response before I was flipped and maneuvered into a position on all fours. My cock hung heavy between my legs, one hundred percent ready for another round. My arms gave out when his tongue pressed against my hole, working me up into a frenzy.

"Such a tight pink hole. All for me. Right, Kalen? Tell me this is mine." Teeth sank into my ass cheek and I cursed.

"You completely own me, Monroe Jackson. Now, fuck my ass before I die."

He barked a laugh. "Wow, that was dramatic." The sound of the bottle of lube opening ramped up my anticipation and when the first drop hit my warm skin, I jolted. Monroe didn't waste any time, working me open and making sure this was going to be something I remembered forever.

"Need to see your face." I chased his fingers as he pulled them from me, and then kissed his way up the center of my back. "Please, Monroe."

Looking over my shoulder, all I could see was his hair as he took his sweet time kissing every vertebrae. When he finally got to my shoulder, he hovered just above me, our breaths becoming one.

"I love you." His lips brushed across mine.

My body felt as if it were floating as I fell to the pillows, turning over so I was on my back. He settled between my legs, our kiss intensifying as our cocks pressed against each other.

"Make love to me," I moaned, lifting my ass to give him easier access to where I needed him to slide home.

His forehead pressed to mine, blue eyes shining, he eased into me. It had been a month since I'd felt him like this, and I vowed in that moment to never let that happen again.

"Are you okay?" He caressed my cheek as he bottomed out and lay still for me to adjust.

"I will be." I grabbed his other hand, entwining our fingers as he began moving with small rolls of his hips. "Mmm, just like that."

His lips found mine again as our bodies connected in the most intimate way I'd ever felt. With every stroke of his cock and brush of his lips, I flew higher and higher until my balls were pulling close to my body.

"Baby, when you clench around me, my own ass clenches and it feels so fucking amazing." His face was buried in my neck as his pace increased.

"Never leave me again, Monroe." I hooked a leg around him, taking him deeper. "Promise me."

"I promise you. Fuck, Kalen. I'll promise you

every minute of every day for the rest of my life." He kissed every part of my face as his thrusts got faster and faster. "Wrap your hand around your cock, baby."

Moving my hand between us, I wrapped my fingers around my shaft and stroked myself at the same pace he was fucking me. Our bodies were slick with sweat, skin slapping together as we chased our orgasms.

"Monroe!" My cock exploded and my ass clenched around him, drawing a cry from his throat as he released inside me.

As we both trembled with the last of our orgasms, the only thing I could see was him.

He was it for me.

EPILOGUE

Monroe

"Jesus, babe. You'd think you were the one waiting to find out your fate." Kalen turned around on the couch and rested his chin on his arms, staring up at me with amused green eyes. "Come relax."

I was wearing a path in the hardwood floor from pacing for the last fifteen minutes. My stomach was in knots, and I was starting to sweat as the start time of the draft drew closer and closer.

Our living room was filled with family and friends, all anxiously awaiting to find out what team was going to pick up Kalen. This time around, things were different for him.

After recovering fully from the accident, he'd hit

his workouts and practices harder than ever. Not just for himself, but for Baker as well. It helped that Baker had threatened multiple times to kick him in the balls if he didn't get his act together.

And get his act together, he did. He'd graduated and was now looking at a first round draft pick because of all his hard work. I was so proud of my man that I found myself alternating between grinning from ear to ear and having to leave the room to stop myself from bawling like a baby.

"I'm just nervous. You've worked so hard, and what if something happens and they don't—" He silenced me by getting to his knees on the couch, grabbing my shirt, and kissing me.

"Get a room," Martinez groaned, pulling us out of our bubble.

"Oh, leave the boys alone," Carol teased, taking a sip of her wine. "It's a shame Baker couldn't be here."

"Yeah, but we're real life adults and shit now. Plus, I think it's hard for him." Kalen sighed and sat back on the couch. "He said he'd be watching. There's always a possibility it won't happen today anyway."

So many teams had taken notice of Kalen that since graduating weeks ago, he'd been traveling around to different camps he was invited to. Plus, there were the calls asking him what he'd accept for offers.

"I learned last year not to count my chickens before they hatch." His voice shook slightly and he squeezed my arm. "Come sit next to me, it's starting."

My heart was in my throat as I rounded our couch and sat next to him, grabbing his hand.

"We're thinking what? Top ten?" Nikki was on the other side of Kalen, a beer in one hand, her girlfriend's hand in the other. "I would be surprised if he goes outside the top ten with all the media attention and biography stuff they've been having him do. Last time they didn't do that."

"Don't jinx it." Kalen elbowed her and put his chin on my shoulder, lowering his voice. "What if I get drafted by New York or somewhere far away?"

"Then we're moving to New York, baby." I squeezed his hand. "Wherever you end up, I'll be there."

Our eyes and ears were glued to the television as the draft announcements started. After each selection, the stats and bio of the chosen player came across the screen, which led to more talking. Couldn't they just save all that for later? Then there were the commercials, which made it even worse.

"I wonder if Barry is watching right now," Carol said softly.

"Who cares what that fucker is doing—we're better off without him." Kalen put his head on my shoulder as they announced the first pick. "You're better off without him."

"I know. I don't know what I would have done if it hadn't been for you two." Carol took another sip of wine, the emotions she was feeling evident in her eyes.

After Kalen's accident, she'd revealed a lot about her relationship with Kalen's father, and how it had evolved into two bodies coexisting in the same household. Once she'd gotten on her feet again with the help of Kalen's sisters, she'd filed for divorce.

"I'm proud of you, Mom." Kalen reached across the coffee table and took his mom's hand. "Thank you for everything. All of you. I wouldn't be sitting here waiting to hear my name called without you."

The teams' continued their selections. It was torturous for me, but even more so for Kalen whose leg started bouncing during the fifth pick.

The announcer walked back across the stage and stood in front of the podium. "With the eighth selection of the MLB draft, the Detroit Tigers select Kalen Bishop, a catcher from Alderwood University."

Everyone in the room exploded with cheers and claps, jumping up and hugging. Laughter rang out around us, but my eyes were on my man. I watched him drop his face into his palms for several moments before looking up. Our gazes collided, much like our souls had almost a year ago. Back when I was just a man sitting on a barstool and he was looking to drown out his perceived failure.

My mouth lifted at the corner and I joined in with the clapping. Nikki and Martinez were jumping up and down, Carol was openly crying, but Kalen just focused on me. When his mouth split into a huge smile, I reached my hand out to him.

He stood, closing the distance between us. Our hearts were magnets; our love was a bond that couldn't be broken.

"Hey, mister major leagues," I teased.

"Hey, old man." He grinned. His entire face lit up with happiness and that bone deep satisfaction that comes with achieving a goal.

"You did it," I murmured, grabbing his hands.

His eyes glistened with tears and I pulled him into my arms.

"I did it," he whispered.

"I'm so proud of you, baby." I cupped his cheek and our lips connected. Every time felt like the first time: that swooping sensation in my lower belly, the way my heartbeat raced at that first flick of his tongue against mine.

Catcalls filled the air and whoops of crude encouragement. I broke the kiss with a laugh.

"I love you, Monroe. I don't think I was meant to get drafted last year. We never would've met, and I can't imagine this moment happening without you," Kalen told me, not bothering to lower his voice. I definitely heard Carol and Nikki each throw out an 'awww.'

"I'm not going anywhere, baby. Which is great, because I hear Detroit has the best Coney dogs in all fifty states, maybe even the world."

Everyone laughed as Kalen's mouth dropped open at my open ribbing of him. What I didn't anticipate was him charging me, tossing me over his shoulder, and heading down the hall.

"Thanks for coming, everyone! Party's over! Love you all, lock the door on the way out!" Kalen shouted, and was met with more cheers and whistles.

"What are you doing?" I demanded, unable to stop laughing and slapping his ass since I was in the perfect position for it. He kicked our bedroom door closed behind him and tossed me on the bed.

He stared down at me with hooded eyes and a cocky grin. "I'm gonna make love to the man I love. Strip for me, Professor."

I'd caught Kalen, and I was never letting him go.

Printed in Great Britain
by Amazon